Deanne Anders was reading romance while her friends were still reading Nancy Drew, and she knew she'd hit the jackpot when she found a shelf of romances in her local library. Years later she discovered the fun of writing her own. Deanne lives in Florida, with her husband and their spoiled Pomeranian. During the day she works as a nursing supervisor. With her love of everything medical and romance, writing for Mills & Boon Medical Romance is a dream come true.

Also by Deanne Anders

From Midwife to Mummy
The Surgeon's Baby Bombshell

Discover more at millsandboon.co.uk.

STOLEN KISS
WITH THE
SINGLE MUM

DEANNE ANDERS

MILLS & BOON

First published in Great Britain 2020
by Mills & Boon, an imprint of HarperCollins*Publishers*
1 London Bridge Street, London, SE1 9GF

Large Print edition 2020

© 2020 Denise Chavers

ISBN: 978-0-263-08584-6

This book is dedicated to all the hard-working emergency room nurses, physicians and techs I have the privilege to work with. You amaze me with the care and dedication you show every day. You have one of the hardest jobs in the hospital, but you make it look easy.

Also, a special thanks to CAPT David Olson USNR (ret), for founding the Combat Wounded Warrior Challenge, and to his wife Teresa for her work with the veterans. Your work lives on with the veterans you touched.

CHAPTER ONE

FOUR O'CLOCK IN the morning could be considered the witching hour in any ER, Lacey was sure, but for a hospital smack-dab in the middle of New Orleans, where voodoo and ghost stories were the norm, it seemed especially true.

Not that she really minded the unusual assortment of patients who seemed to find their way into the emergency room at that time of morning. If nothing else it definitely helped pass the last few hours before the sun started peeking through the windows—the first sign that the next shift would be there soon.

Unfortunately, the early-morning hours hadn't seen their usual influx of eclectic patients today, and now the hours till shift-change had begun to drag.

"What's he looking up now?" the young unit coordinator asked.

Lacey looked over to where Scott Boudreaux, one of the on-duty ER doctors, sat studying his computer screen.

"Planning his next adventure, I'm sure," she said.

Lacey had never understood the man's desire to put himself at risk for the thrill of survival, but she had learned she might as well keep her concerns to herself. Hadn't she had almost the same conversations with her husband when he had been alive? And what good had it done her?

The two men had always been more than she could handle, with neither of them ever listening to her concerns. Then they'd both volunteered for that last deployment to Afghanistan and now Ben was gone.

There had been a time when she had blamed Scott for her husband's death, though she had known even then that it was stupid to think that way. Ben had wanted to return and help the injured soldiers on the field as much as Scott. The two of them had been like two peas in a pod through medical school, and she had finally learned to accept their adventures together, thinking the two of them would be safe as long as they were together.

She'd been wrong.

Scott had been lucky to come out with only an injury to his leg after an IED had exploded, but he'd been left with this need to always prove himself. She just couldn't understand why he felt he had to spend his life searching out thrill after thrill. Just the experience of working in the emergency room alone gave her all the taste of adventure that she needed. Add to that the trials of being a single mom and she had all the thrills she could handle.

"The next Extreme Warrior trip is only a couple weeks from now, and I think the winter trip to Alaska is pretty much planned, so he's probably working on the spring trip."

"There's a rumor that they're going to hunt Sasquatch next," the unit coordinator said.

Lacey laughed at the idea of a bunch of war veterans trying to hunt down the mythological hairy creature.

"Now, that *would* be extreme," she said, then looked over to Scott to see his reaction.

"Y'all know I can hear you, right?" Scott said as he glanced over to the two of them and then winked.

The UC let out an audible sigh and Lacey couldn't help but understand why. With his longish blond hair curling around his collar and those unusual gray-green eyes that she had always found to be seductive, he'd broken more than a few of her co-workers' hearts.

"And I'm adding the Sasquatch hunt to my list of possibilities."

Lacey laughed again when the UC's mouth dropped open. Though she knew Scott had meant to tease the girl, she wasn't sure that he wasn't totally serious. He lived to come up with new ways to challenge the group of veterans he worked with. The whole bunch of them were crazy as far as she was concerned.

When Scott had come back from Afghanistan without Ben he'd been just as lost as her. The two of them had struggled through that time together, and when he had first brought up the idea of starting the Extreme Warrior program that he and Ben had been planning before Ben's death she had been supportive.

He'd had no idea how fast the program would grow, with more and more veterans attending the meetings and applying to go on the extreme trips that Scott planned. Now, with the fast growth of the program, Scott was looking for some hands-on help, and had begun pressuring her to join the group.

Though she knew Ben would want her to help his friend in any way she could, in her heart she knew it was Ben who should have been there to help Scott, not her. The memories of sitting around the table with the two of them as they made plans to serve the military veterans in the New Orleans area just reminded her of how much of life Ben had missed out on.

The thought of her husband's death took all the humor she'd felt minutes ago out of her. She'd planned her life so carefully. She'd seen her mother struggle as a single mom, after Lacey's father had walked out on them, and she had sworn then that she'd make a different kind of life when she grew up.

So she'd gone to college and gotten the nursing degree that had allowed her to live independently and she had been happy. Then she'd met Ben, and had known right away that he was a man she could trust her heart with.

When she had married him the thought that she might lose him had never entered her head. He'd been a doctor, not a soldier. He hadn't been supposed to die so young. He hadn't been supposed to leave her with a four-year-old son who couldn't remember his daddy.

The radio on her desk went off and the voice of one of the city's emergency medical technicians began spitting out information concerning the patient they were transporting.

"Patient is a fifty-four-year-old male suffering from multiple injuries, including a laceration to the head. No loss of consciousness after a car versus light post MVA. Vital signs are: heart-rate in the one-tens, BP one-sixty-five over ninety and respirations twenty-four, with an oxygen saturation of ninety-two on five liters oxygen. ETA ten minutes, and arriving with New Orleans Police Department officer on board."

She looked at the room's tracking board, then hit the button on her radio. The EMTs hadn't called the patient in as a trauma, and the patients vital signs were stable, so she didn't want to tie up a trauma bed unnecessarily.

"Room Thirty-Two on arrival," she said, and then got up to get the room ready for the new patient.

"Am I getting a patient?" asked Karen, one of the RNs who regularly worked the night shift, as she walked by.

"No, I'm going to take this one," Lacey said.

The night had been dragging, and the fact that a police officer was aboard the ambulance with the patient might prove to be interesting. She wouldn't mind a little excitement to help the last hours of her shift pass by. She'd spent too much time tonight thinking about things she couldn't change.

At the sound of Lacey's laughter Scott pushed back from his desk and looked down the hall to where she stood with one of the other nurses. Unlike the high-pitched giggle of some of the women he had dated, Lacey's laugh had always been genuine.

It had been her laughter that had caught his attention the first time he'd seen her. With her head of dark red hair thrown back and her bright green eyes shining with humor, she'd been a vision. Never had he seen someone actually glow with happiness till that night. He'd known then that she was one of a kind, and only the fact that his best friend had laid claim to her first had kept him from pursuing her.

But she wasn't the same woman she'd been then. She was older now, more mature, yet still just as beautiful as the first day he had set eyes on her. Life had knocked her down with Ben's death, but she'd managed to get back up. It had been hard, and there had been a time when he had thought he would never hear her laughter again, which only made the sound of her laugh sweeter to his ears now.

If only his best friend was there to hear it.

As it always did when he thought of

Ben, guilt slammed through him. He'd never understand why it had been him who had made it home and not Ben, who'd had a wife and son waiting for him. He knew it should have been Ben who had survived.

Watching as Lacey continued walking down to the back of the unit, he wondered if she ever thought the same thing. Did those thoughts haunt her as they did him?

Turning back to his computer, he pushed thoughts of his friend's death to the back of his mind so that he could return his focus to work. After checking the lab work on the elderly patient who was next to be seen, he picked up the man's chart and headed down the hall.

Lacey had just gotten the room stocked with the suture supplies she thought Scott would need when the ambulance crew rolled in with their patient, and a tired-looking police officer on their tail. The smell of alcohol hit her before she could even get a glance at the patient, which was enough to explain the presence of the officer.

"Thanks, Larry," she said to one of the techs as he came in, and they both assisted the EMTs in transferring the man over to the stretcher. The patient remained unresponsive as they moved him. Whether that was from the accident or the alcohol intoxication she couldn't tell.

She hooked the patient up to all the monitors and noted that the man's heart-rate and other vital signs appeared to have deteriorated from when she had gotten the initial report. She began checking the man's body for injuries. There was a cut above his right eye that oozed blood. It would need a few stitches. But her real concern was the possibility of a traumatic head injury due to whatever the man had hit his head on during the MVA.

She mentally moved the man to the top of the list of patients who needed to go to Radiology to get a CAT scan. They'd need his chest and abdomen scanned as well as his head.

"You said he didn't lose consciousness at first?" she asked the EMT who'd remained in the room, and was now filling out the needed paperwork.

"Not that we're aware of. He was awake when we got there. He passed out on the way here," he said. "His alcohol level has to be at least in the three hundreds."

She walked back over to the stretcher and rubbed the man's sternum hard enough to get a response. The man moaned and one bloodshot eye opened. He looked around the room, moaned again, and closed the eye. So he did respond to pain. But still those vital signs bothered her.

"Name?" she asked.

"James Lyons," the EMT read off his paperwork, then tore the form from his pad, handed her a copy, and walked out the door.

She looked over at the police officer who had taken a spot by the door.

"What are you charging him with?" she asked him.

"DUI," the man said. "Along with property damage and driving with a suspended license. He swiped the side of a car before he hit the light pole. It's not his first DUI. He served time for his last one. If someone had been sitting in the car he sideswiped they'd be dead now."

"Mr. Lyons, can you hear me? I need you to wake up for me."

This time the man opened both his eyes. Hopefully his unresponsiveness earlier had more to do with his alcohol consumption than injury. Or the man could be playing possum instead of dealing with the police officer in the room. She didn't have enough information to know yet.

"Do you hurt anywhere?" she asked as she shone a light into his eyes. His pupils were reactive, but she still felt there was more to his injuries than what she was seeing.

The man moaned, then grabbed his left

side and looked over to the corner, where the cop was now sitting. Looking at the monitor, Lacey noticed that his oxygen saturations had dropped again, and his respirations had increased too. Pulling her stethoscope from around her neck, she placed the chest-piece against his chest and listened He was definitely moving less air on the left side.

"If you can get a line in for me, Larry, and draw the standard labs, I'd appreciate it. I'll go get some orders from Dr. Boudreaux and then we'll get over to CT," she said, as she turned the patient's oxygen up, then started out of the room. "And can you keep an eye on those vitals too? If there's any change just call me on my radio."

Not seeing Scott at his desk, she went in search of him in one of his patients' rooms and found him sitting on a stool having a conversation with an elderly man. The man's hair was pure white, his body thin and bent with age, but his smile lit his wrinkled face and his eyes sparkled with pleasure.

"Lacey, come in here," Scott said when he saw her. "I want you to meet Lieutenant Hines. He was in Europe in World War Two."

"It's nice to meet you, Lieutenant Hines," she said to the elderly man, who seemed to be embarrassed from all the attention he was getting.

"It's Frank, Miss Lacey," he said. "My days of being a lieutenant are long gone."

"It's nice meeting you, Frank," she said.

She hated to interrupt Scott, but she knew he would be tied up here for a while, talking to and examining this patient. She needed to get her new patient to CT as soon as possible, and with the increase of his oxygen needs she didn't have time to wait till he was finished.

"Can I speak to you for a minute, Dr. Boudreaux?" she asked.

"Sure. I'll be right back with you," Scott

told the elderly patient before he left the room with her.

"The man's almost one hundred years old, but his mind is sharp. The things he saw were amazing," Scott said.

"What's he here for?" she asked as they moved away from the door.

"Blood sugar was reported low at his assisted living home. It's coming up, but his electrolytes are off so I'm going to admit him and get those corrected. He lost his wife over ten years ago, and they never had any children, so he's alone except for a niece who lives in California," Scott said.

He couldn't have been in the room more than fifteen minutes, but he already knew the man's life history. It never failed to amaze her how he could get people to talk to him. When depression had all but consumed her after Ben's death, and she'd been at her lowest, not only had Scott gotten her to a counselor, he'd sat beside her for hours and just let her talk. It was a gift that made him not only a good doctor, but also a great friend.

"I didn't mean to interrupt, but I've got a patient who just rolled in and I'm thinking he possibly should have been trauma-alerted. I'm putting in orders for the usual labs, but he's got a laceration on his forehead that's going to need some stitches and I've ordered a scan of his head. Can you take a look at him for me?" she asked.

"Why do you think he should have been trauma-alerted? His head injury?" he asked.

"Maybe. He's requiring more oxygen than he needed when the EMTs arrived," she said. "He's heavily intoxicated, but there's something else going on too."

"Order a portable X-ray for me. I'll be finished here in just a minute and then I'll head straight there."

She watched as he returned to the elderly man's room. She noticed that his limp was more pronounced than it normally was, but she wasn't surprised as this was the last of seven straight days on duty. The injury to his leg that he'd received in Afghanistan hadn't slowed him down a bit, and he had never let it stop him, but sometimes she wished he would. She'd have a lot fewer gray hairs if he'd slow down and quit running around the world chasing the next thrill.

She turned back toward her patient's room as she called on her radio to have the X-ray tech come down.

Scott reviewed the vital signs on the monitor, then walked over to the man lying on the stretcher as Lacey laid out the chest tube kit. While the CT scans had ruled out any brain injury, they had shown a significant pneumothorax, proving Lacey had been right to be concerned about the patient's vital signs changes and his decreased breath sounds.

Not that it surprised him. He'd been working with her long enough now to know he could trust her instincts.

"Mr. Lyons, I'm Dr. Boudreaux. You have several rib fractures from the accident and one of them has punctured your left lung, which is affecting your breathing. I'm going to need to insert a chest tube."

The man didn't seem to be paying much attention to what he was saying. Instead he seemed to be more interested in Lacey and the tray of instruments that she was setting up.

"Don't let those instruments scare you. I'm going to inject some lidocaine to numb the site on your chest where I'll insert the tube. You shouldn't feel anything," he said, and he turned toward the sink in the room and began to wash his hands.

Something crashed behind him and he turned back, expecting to see that Lacey had bumped into the stand that held the instruments. Instead he saw the patient he'd just been explaining the procedure to standing beside the bed, holding Lacey against him. The glint of steel caught his eye and he realized that the man had a scalpel in his hand.

As if he had just stepped through a time warp, he was suddenly thrown back into the war zone of Afghanistan, standing in the quickly thrown-up field hospital…

There was chaos everywhere he looked as nurses and doctors worked on the wounded who had just arrived. He looked up and saw Ben standing in front of him. Another man held a knife to his throat while he shouted to them in a language Scott didn't understand.

Ben told him that the man had an IED, and then he watched as suddenly Ben went down and everything exploded.

He heard screams coming from all around him, and knew one of the screams was his own. A piece of metal had torn into his leg as he was thrown under one of the operating tables.

Then he heard only silence, and it took a moment for him to realize that the blast of the explosion had damaged his ears.

He crawled through the rubble, dragging his injured leg behind him as he looked for Ben. He could see the wounded as they cried out for help, but still could not hear a sound.

He made it over to where his friend lay, pulling him into his lap and propping the two of them against the side of a turned-over table. As tears rolled down his own face he tried to wipe away the blood from his friend's face.

Ben turned, his eyes no longer bright with life, And Scott watched as his friend worked laboriously to speak, concentrating on the movement of his friend's lips as he slowly formed words.

"Lacey and Alston," his friend said. "Take care of them for me."

"Always," Scott answered before his friend's eyes closed for the last time. "Always."

The tray stand crashed to the floor and just as quickly as he'd disappeared into the nightmare that still haunted his sleep he was back, watching as the man, now totally out of control, wrecked his emergency room and threatened his best friend's wife.

He took a deep breath and tried to slow his speeding heart. He didn't have time to deal with his own demons now. He had to get this situation under control before Lacey was hurt. He wouldn't let Lacey or Ben down again.

"Whoa, man, you don't want to do this," Scott said as he slowly approached the wild-eyed man.

The man's trembling hand tightened around the scalpel he held against Lacey's throat.

Scott stopped moving and held up his hands with his palms facing forward, showing the man they were empty, letting the man know he wasn't a threat. He had to find some way to get through to this guy before he hurt her.

He looked from the man's hands to

Lacey's pale face. She'd gone so still he wasn't sure she was even breathing. Her green eyes were wide with a look of fear that he was only too familiar with. He'd seen it on a countless number of injured soldiers. He'd seen it on Ben's face just before that insurgent had detonated the bomb he'd been wearing. It killed him to see it on Lacey's face now.

Then her eyes caught his and her lips moved.

Alston, she mouthed, and the word was as plain to him as if she had spoken it. *Take care of Alston.*

No. He couldn't live through this again. Nothing was going to happen to Lacey. He wouldn't let it.

Did she think he was just going to stand there and let this guy hurt her? Kill her? He'd lost too many people in his life already. He would not lose Lacey. There had to be a way to get this man to let her go.

"Look, I don't know your story," he said to the man as he moved an inch closer, "but I do know that woman you're holding, and I know that whatever is going on that has driven you to do something like this is not her fault."

Scott slowly moved closer to the man. The police officer who had been with them earlier took a step into the room from the other side, causing the man to jerk Lacey up closer to him as he tightened his hand around the scalpel at her throat. One slice to her jugular and she'd bleed out before Scott could save her.

"Don't come any closer. I don't want to hurt her, but I'm not going back to jail," the man said. "I want a car outside in fifteen minutes or…"

Scott watched as the man struggled for breath. Was his color a bit cyanotic? If he could keep the man talking long enough he'd pass out with hypoxia. Only that would still leave the sharp scalpel dangerously close to Lacey's neck when the man went down…

"Do you see how short of breath you

are? You need to stay here in the hospital so that we can treat you."

"She's a nurse." The man gestured with the hand that held the scalpel. "She can take care of me."

Scott had to get through to this man *now*. It would help if he knew something about him, but he only remembered the basic information. He couldn't even remember the man's name now. All he knew was that Lacey was in danger and he was going to have to get her out of it without her being hurt.

He watched as the man's hand began to shake again. He had to do something—and now. He would *not* lose someone he cared about again.

"Her name's Lacey and she's one of the best nurses I've ever worked with," Scott said as he moved closer.

He made himself look the man in the eyes, all the while thinking about the sharp scalpel lying against Lacey's neck. His instincts told him to grab her and run, but his training told him that would put her at risk. He had to talk this man down if he was going to have any chance of keeping her safe.

"She's caring and professional and she treats everyone with respect, no matter what their background. But you'd already know that, wouldn't you?" Scott said.

The man's eyes left his and he looked down at Lacey.

Scott took another step—a larger one this time. "She's also one of the best moms I've ever known. She does that thing where she leaves notes in her son's lunchbox. Not mushy notes. The kid's eight and she knows better than that. Instead she writes down corny jokes that he reads to his friends every day at lunch," Scott said, and made a sound as close to a laugh as he could manage.

Yep, there's no threat here. I'm just a simple doctor having a conversation with his patient...

The man had gone quiet now, though

whether it was from listening to him or from the lack of oxygen going to his brain Scott didn't know. But as the scalpel had moved a fraction of an inch away from Lacey's neck he really didn't care which.

Scott saw the police officer behind the man moving closer. The officer had his Taser out, but he wouldn't be able to use it until Lacey was free. They had the man boxed in now—he wouldn't be leaving with Lacey—but they didn't want him to realize that yet.

"The boy lost his dad in Afghanistan, so Lacey's the only parent he has. He's got his momma's red-haired temper, but he's a good kid and he needs his mom," Scott said, and took one more step closer to Lacey.

She was within arm's reach now. The officer behind the man nodded his head. It was time for this to end.

"Like I said, I don't know your story, but I do know that whatever or whoever you have a problem with, it's not Lacey's fault. Let her go and we can talk. Please," Scott said, as he held out his hands toward the man, "just let her go."

"I don't wanna hurt nobody," the man said, his voice slurred and tears filling his eyes. "I just wanna go home."

The officer behind the man nodded one more time. It was now or never.

Scott reached out his hand for Lacey's, felt it tremble as she laid it in his, and with one motion yanked her into his arms.

Police and Security surrounded the man as his body collapsed and convulsed from being Tasered.

CHAPTER TWO

LACEY CLUNG TO SCOTT. Nothing had ever felt as good as being held safe in his arms right then. She'd heard many a trauma survivor talk about having their lives flash before them, but she'd never experienced anything like that until now. With the sharp edge of the scalpel lying against her neck, fear had taken over her body, and with it had come the knowledge that she might have seen her little boy for the last time.

The adrenaline rush she had experienced earlier was gone now and her body had started to tremble. She looked around the hallway Scott had pulled her into. Had it all been real? Her body wanted to crumple there on the floor and curl into itself, protect her from the fear that was flooding through her.

She remembered another time when that had happened—when the chaplain from the base had told her about Ben's death. She'd sunk to the floor that day and had never wanted to get up. She'd had to fight her way up every day after that, taking it one hour at a time, then one day, one week. At first she had failed more than she'd succeeded, but with counseling, and support from her family and friends, she'd finally gotten to where she was today.

The possibility of becoming that broken woman again scared her more than that scalpel against her neck.

She gave her head a hard shake and pushed away from Scott. "I need some air," she said, then headed for the exit door.

Outside, the sky was still dark, but from where she stood she could see the city starting to come to life. Lights began to come on all around her as the early shift workers began to prepare for the day.

She leaned against the wall that enclosed the roof and for the first time in her life wished for a cigarette to hold in her shaking hands. The façade she had held on to until she'd been able to make her escape fell, and with it the tears she could no longer hold inside.

Alone in the dark, she let the tears fall as she stared out into the city. She couldn't let anyone see her like this. She had her reputation as a hard-nosed ER nurse to uphold. Laughter broke through her sobs. Some kick-ass nurse she had turned out to be.

"Lacey?"

She heard a voice call into the shadows where she hid. She mopped at the tears with the sleeve of her jacket, but she didn't answer—couldn't speak at all while she worked to hold the sobs inside her. What would Scott the mighty thrill-seeker think of her hiding in the dark, crying like some scared little rookie nurse?

She wiped at her tears again as Scott walked into her hiding place and then pulled her into his arms. The dam broke and she let the tears and the sobs take over.

"I was so scared," she said, speaking between sobs against his shoulder. "If something happened to me… Alston would be all alone…"

"It's okay," Scott said. "You're okay."

She knew that, but still she cried.

"I know. It's just…" she said.

Scott's hand ran up and down her back, his touch soothing her. Her body began to relax, her breaths becoming less ragged and her heart-rate slowing. Scott whispered in her ear, sweet sounds that calmed her fears. She was safe here with him.

She knew she needed to move away from him, in case someone saw them and took what was simply the act of comforting a friend as something less innocent, but she couldn't move, couldn't leave the warmth of his body. A body that was strong and safe...one that fit so perfectly with hers. A hard body that was starting to send all kinds of tingles through hers.

Wait. Something was wrong. This was Scott. Her friend. Her late husband's best friend. There could be no tingles between the two of them.

Lacey started to push away, but Scott only pulled her closer. One of his hands cupped her face, turning it up toward him, his green-gray eyes captured hers filled with desperation.

"I would never let anything happen to you, Lacey," he promised as he looked down at her.

She knew he was going to kiss her a second before he lowered his head. She could have turned her face, could have pushed away from him, but his eyes— so earnest—seemed to hold her in place until his lips were on hers and then it was too late. There was no fighting the warm touch of his lips as they met hers.

She had felt so cold and alone before Scott had found her. Now the heat from his body drove the cold away and his arms around her reminded her that she was no longer alone. Her mouth opened and his tongue swept in, scattering all reason from her mind as desire crowded out the fear that had held her prisoner earlier.

In the back of her mind an alarm warned her. But of what she could no longer remember. Right now there was just her and this blessed kiss, which reminded her that she was alive and safe as long as she remained in the strong arms that held her.

She tasted of sunshine and hope and everything that he had been afraid of losing as he'd watched her stand there so still with that scalpel held against her throat. If that man had hurt her…if he had lost her…there would have been no hope left in his life.

He poured everything he had into the kiss, trying to reassure himself that she was real, that she was alive and safe. Her body relaxed into his, melting into him, and then he felt himself harden against her and realized he had taken things a little too far. What had started out as a need to confirm that Lacey was alive and safe had turned into a desire that he had never let himself acknowledge before.

He felt her stiffen against him and knew she had felt the change too. He eased out of the kiss, withdrawing slowly until there was a small sliver of space between them.

She blinked up at him with eyes that went from startled to horrified in a second then stared at him as if she had never seen him before.

But then she had never seen this side of him, had she? Even though the two of them were close, they'd always been careful to keep their relationship free of anything that could be interpreted as something other than friendship.

"This never happened," Lacey whispered, then backed away from him.

"Wait," he said as she continued to put space between the two of them. "We need to talk."

"No, I have to go. I've got patients. I need to call the lab."

He started toward her as she stumbled, but she held her hands up to stop him.

"Don't. I just need to go," she said, and she turned away from him and hurried toward the stairs.

He watched as she all but ran from him. What had he been thinking? He'd crossed that invisible line that lay between friends and lovers—a line that no one ever crossed without there being consequences to their relationship. A line he had never dreamed he would cross.

For the second time that day time stood still for him—except that this time, instead of a nightmare, it had felt more like a dream come true.

But nothing could happen between him

and Lacey. He'd promised her husband that he would take care of her and Alston and that promise had never included anything but friendship. A friend didn't make moves on his dead friend's wife. That was just not done.

He turned east and watched the sun as it rose across the sky, creating a work of art with its blend of pinks, purples and blues that no human artist could ever truly copy. The night was over and a new day was beginning. Each day was as unique as its sunrise, and he'd learned the hard way that no one knew when a day began how it would end.

He lived his life with the motto that you had to live each day as if it was your last. There were no promises of tomorrow. You had to make the life you wanted now, because today was all you could count on till the sun began to rise again.

Only sometimes life came with unexpected complications that you weren't prepared for—and the kiss he had just shared with Lacey was one big complication.

He headed back to the ER. Maybe he should have fought off the need he'd had to kiss Lacey, but he'd needed to reassure himself that she was alive and with him at that moment.

He'd explain it to her. They'd been friends for a long time and he would never have purposely done anything to threaten that friendship. Surely she wouldn't let one kiss in the heat of the moment ruin what they had between the two of them? They were both adults and it had only been one kiss. Just one kiss.

But what a kiss it had been.

Lacey tried to pay attention to the convoluted story her eight-year-old was telling her, but her mind kept wandering back to the last shift she'd worked. She'd been able to throw off the fear that had seized her the night before after she'd gotten some sleep, thank goodness. And she'd mostly managed to file the experience with the intoxicated patient in the back of her mind, with all the other memories she hoped to forget someday.

Now she found that it wasn't the fact that she had been held hostage with a cold scalpel against her neck that occupied her mind. Instead it was what had happened later, between her and Scott. What had he…she…*they* been thinking?

They'd both been recovering from a flood of adrenaline. They'd both been scared and had needed reassurance that the two of them were safe. She could even have pushed the line a little, with the two of them sharing a hug, a kiss on the cheek, but that kiss…

That hadn't been the kiss of two friends, sharing their fear of what might have been. No, that kiss had definitely *not* been a kiss between two friends.

The feel of her fingers against her lips broke through her daydreaming and she jerked them away. Scott would be here at

any minute, to take Alston to soccer practice, and she didn't need him to think she
was obsessing over a kiss that had meant
nothing to either one of them.

"And then Ms. Little told me to leave the
class and never come back," Alston said.

"What?" she said.

She caught the glass of milk her hand
had hit before it toppled over, then sent
her son her most intimidating Mommy
stare.

"Alston Benjamin Miller—what did you
say?" She watched as Alston's face broke
out into a grin.

"Gotcha!" he said, then jumped down
from his seat and began dancing around
in a circle, making sounds that reminded
her of an injured cow.

Marching around the corner of the
counter, she grabbed her son up in her
arms and squeezed. He was her life, her
everything. If anything ever happened
to him…

She squeezed him tighter as he made

fake choking sounds. He looked up at her and she thought her heart would stop. He'd been born with her red hair and green eyes, but that mischievous smile with its pair of dimples had come straight from Ben. He was growing up so fast and there was nothing she could do to slow the time down.

She gave him another squeeze, then put him back down. "I'm sorry," she said, "I should have been paying more attention."

"It's okay," Alston said.

"Tonight we'll order pizza and you can tell me the whole story again."

The doorbell rang, which sent him running for the door.

"Slow down!" she called after him.

She caught herself questioning her choice of shorts and an old hospital T-shirt. What was wrong with her? One kiss with a man and all of a sudden she was making a fool of herself. This had to stop now. She'd been kissed many times before she'd met Ben.

But you've haven't been kissed since Ben.

Her mind froze on that thought. Was the problem she was having with the memory of kissing Scott as simple as that? If so, then this strange quiver she had in her stomach at the thought of seeing him would surely go away soon.

She had just loaded the last glass into the dishwasher when Alston and Scott came into the room.

"Hurry and grab your shoes," she said to her son. "You don't want to keep Scott waiting."

She tried to make her eyes look up at Scott, but instead she busied herself wiping down the counters. She turned her back to him to clean the stove top, and then stopped. She was acting like an immature teenager instead of the mature single mom that she was.

Turning around to face Scott, she pasted her most friendly smile on her face—the one she used when a patient was really annoying, but she knew she had to play nice.

"You okay? I'm sorry that happened yesterday," Scott said as he moved over to where Alston had dropped his soccer bag. He grabbed the bag, then moved to the counter. "I started to call last night, to check on you, but I didn't want to wake you. I figured you'd have had a hard time sleeping. I know I did."

Did he really want to talk about this now? Where did they start?

You shouldn't have kissed me?

I shouldn't have kissed you back?

What did he mean, he'd had a hard time sleeping? Had thinking of that kiss kept him awake like it had her? Did he have the same strange quiver in his stomach that she had? And he wanted to talk about it *now*? No, that couldn't be what he meant. They had to put that kiss behind them. They had a great relationship and they couldn't afford to lose it.

"We can't do that again," she said, then squeezed her eyes shut. Why couldn't her mouth get on track with her mind? She took a deep breath, then opened her eyes. "What I meant to say is that I think it would be best if you didn't kiss me again."

"Um… Lacey, I was talking about that patient grabbing you and trying to take you hostage," Scott said, his eyes now looking away from her.

Of *course* he was talking about the patient with the scalpel. He probably hadn't given the kiss they'd shared another thought. The man probably went around kissing women all the time. What would one kiss shared with a friend mean to him?

They both looked up as Alston came back into the room.

"Why'd someone grab you?" Alston asked, hands on his hips as if he was preparing to interrogate her.

Scott gave her a guilty smile, then ran his hand over her son's ginger hair. "Nothing for you to worry about," he told the boy, who was now making a show of studying the two of them.

"If someone hurt my mom I'll punch them in the nose," Alston said, and he brought his small fist up and shook it.

She watched as Scott's lips twitched and they both held back laughter.

"Mikey said his big brother punched his sister's boyfriend in the nose. He said there was blood everywhere. Mikey's mom got mad about the blood and made his brother apologize to the jerk."

"Jerk?" she asked.

"Yeah, that's what Mikey called him. Was it a jerk that grabbed you?" he asked her.

"It was definitely a jerk," Scott said. "But the cops took care of him so you don't need to punch him."

She could see that her son was ready to argue the point and she wasn't prepared for that now.

Alston took his position as the "man" of the house very seriously. He'd begun by taking out the garbage, though at first that had been more of a mess than if she had done it herself, but she'd known it made him feel like he was helping out so she'd watched him drag the trash bag out through the back door and then hurried to clean up the mess he'd left on the floor before he could return and see it.

"Y'all better get going or you're going to be late for practice," she reminded the two of them.

"Let's go," Scott said, and he wrapped his arm around her son's shoulder as they headed for the door.

"Oh, and about that other thing… If you want to talk about it later we can," Scott said, though from the tight expression on his face she knew he would prefer not to talk about it.

"There's nothing to talk about. Everything's good. We're good, right?" she asked, and held her breath waiting for his answer.

"Yeah, sure. We're good," Scott said, and he hurried out the door with her son without looking back at her.

She took in a deep breath as the front door shut. The man was certainly not going to make this easy for her. And it was entirely that kiss's fault.

CHAPTER THREE

WITHOUT THE BUFFER of Alston between the two of them Lacey and Scott had fallen into an awkward pattern of nods and one-word comments, which were not making their work situation a good one.

She looked over at him now, as he carefully numbed her patient's arm. While most teenagers would have been looking away or turning pale on seeing the long needle, this kid was totally enthralled by the scene.

Scott reached for the suture she had prepared for him just as she reached for a four-by-four, and their hands touched for a second before they both pulled back as if burnt, the motion sending the tray stand rocking precariously.

Grabbing the stand support, she steadied

the tray, then looked over at Scott. "Sorry, I'm a bit clumsy today," she said, as she tried to cover the new self-consciousness she felt when they were this close.

Scott acknowledged her comment with another of his nods before he reached again for the suture and carefully sewed the cut closed.

"Wow! Mom, are you watching this?" asked Kevin, their patient. "This is sick."

"No, Kevin. I do not want to watch," the boy's mother answered back "And you're right. Anyone who'd want to watch *is* sick."

Lacey looked over to where the woman sat on an old plastic chair that had been pushed into the corner when she had brought the tray stand into the room. The woman, who had been handling her son's skateboard wreck well enough when they had first arrived, was now pale and dia-phoretic.

Lacey felt like kicking herself. If she hadn't been so absorbed in her own feelings she would have seen this coming sooner.

Leaving the boy's side, she went over to where the woman was now hunched over with her head down between her legs. Kneeling beside her, Lacey ripped open an alcohol swab package and handed it to her.

"This will help some. I'll get you a washcloth. Dr. Boudreaux is almost finished," Lacey said.

The woman looked up and gave her a weak smile. "I'm sorry about this. I've never had a problem before," she said.

"I'll tell you a secret, but don't tell any of the other staff members," Lacey said as she moved closer to the woman. "I can handle the most gory trauma patients that come in here, but if my son gets a cut I have to call Dr. Boudreaux to handle it every time. It's just different when it's your kid that's hurt."

"Yeah, it is," the woman said.

Lacey noticed that some of her color was back and she had started to sit up now.

"Okay, I'm finished," Scott said. "Kevin, you are one tough kid. Maybe you should think about being a surgeon when you grow up."

"Maybe," Kevin said. "It would be real cool to be able to sew people up. But I'm more interested in electronics. Especially robots."

"They are pretty cool. Did you know they're using them in surgery now?" Scott said. "Someday it might be a robot stitching you up."

The boy's eyes grew big and his mother rolled her eyes.

"Let's not plan on getting any more stitches," she mother said as she moved from the chair to the exam table.

She thanked Scott, then turned to Lacey when he'd left the room.

"He's a very nice man," she said to Lacey, "and good with kids."

"Yes, he is," Lacey said.

"And he's hot, too," the woman said.

Lacey laughed as Kevin moaned at his

mother's comment, and then excused herself so that she could get the necessary discharge paperwork. As she walked back to the nurses' station she saw one of the security guards heading her way.

"Hey, Lacey!" Karen called to her. "We need some help."

"What's up?" Lacey asked, as she signed on to her computer.

"There's an elderly man in the lobby who insists his wife works here, but I've called all the units and all the offices are closed," the guard stated.

"He doesn't know where his wife works?" Lacey asked as she worked to finish up Kevin's paperwork.

"That's it—he seems very confused and I don't know what to do with him," Karen said. "He can't give me an address or a phone number so that I can call his family. I'd feel better if you could check him out for me."

Lacey looked up at the large screen

hanging over the station. They were busy, but there were still a few open rooms.

"Take him to Fifteen and I'll come by as soon as I get this discharge done," she said.

Lacey finished the discharge, then headed to Room Fifteen. She'd worked with Karen long enough to know she wouldn't have asked for help unless she had legitimate concerns.

An elderly man with mocha skin and snow-white hair sat in the chair next to where Karen stood. He was dressed in gray striped dress pants and a white button-up shirt with the sleeves rolled above his elbows. The fact that he was clean and well-dressed told her that the man was not homeless—or at least hadn't been homeless for very long.

"Lacey, this is Mr. Myers," Karen said. "Mr. Myers, this is Lacey. She's the charge nurse on duty right now."

The man stood and offered Lacey his hand.

"Can you help me find my Janie?" the man asked after they shook hands.

"I'm not sure, but I'll try," Lacey said. "Karen says that your wife works here at the hospital. Do you know what she does here?"

Lacey found it hard to believe that this man's wife would still be working, if she was near his age, but they did have some older volunteers who worked at the hospital. She watched as the man tried to work through her question. She could see his frustration and understood why Karen had brought him to her.

"I tell you what, let's work through this another way. If you can give me your first name and your date of birth I can go check our records. Maybe then I can get a phone number, and we can call her and let her know you're here to see her."

To her relief the man rattled off his birthdate without any trouble.

"And your first name?"

"Pop," the man said.

"Pop?" she asked.

"Yes, they call me Pop," he said.

"I'm going to go see what I can find out. Can you wait here for me? I'll try not to be long."

The man agreed, then sat down in the chair. She noticed for the first time the small bouquet of daisies held in the man's hand. Hoping she'd be able to pull up his information in the hospital data bank, she went back to the nurses' station.

She caught herself looking over at Scott, where he sat across from her, working on his own computer. She thought about what the woman had said before she'd left and she had to agree. Scott was hot.

He'd let his hair grow out since he'd come home from Afghanistan, and he'd pulled it back today into a stubby ponytail. She'd joked with him last week about him growing out a man bun, pulling it back from his face to show him that he was close to having enough hair to put it up. But that had been before the kiss that had made things awkward between the two of them. Somehow that now seemed too intimate.

She was letting that stupid kiss, that hot and toe-curling kiss, ruin everything. All she wanted was for things to go back to the way they had been before they'd muddled things up.

Using the frustration that filled her, she hammered the keys of her keyboard. Right now she needed to be more concerned with finding information on Mr. Myers than how she was going to work things out between her and Scott.

"What's wrong?" Scott said from behind her.

Jumping, Lacey swore, and then turned her chair around to face him.

"Excuse me?" she said.

She heard the anger in her voice and stopped. This was not the way to fix things between the two of them.

"I'm sorry. I'm just frustrated," she said. "I'm trying to find some information so I can call this man's family, but he can't tell me his phone number or where he lives. He says his name is Pop, which has to be a nickname. It's probably what his grandkids call him. Not surprisingly, I can't find anything under the name Pop Myers."

"Pop Myers? *The* Pop Myers?" Scott said, and smiled for the first time that day.

"You know him?" she asked.

"I know *of* him," Scott said. "He's an amazing blues and jazz piano player."

"That's great, but what I need right now is a number or an address for where he lives. His wife is probably out looking for him," Lacey said as she turned back to her computer screen.

"Hold on," Scott said. "I think I know someone who can help."

Lacey watched as Scott pulled out his phone and started going through his contacts. This was the Scott she knew. The Scott she was comfortable with. The take-charge-and-make-it-work Scott.

Leaving the mystery of Pop's family in Scott's hands, Lacey went to the waiting room to call her next patient to be examined. Peeking into Pop's room as she ushered an elderly woman who was suffering from shortness of breath down the hall, she saw that he was sound asleep in his chair, his respirations even. And although he looked a bit uncomfortable, she thought it was safe to leave him alone for a little bit longer.

After getting her new patient a stat breathing treatment and ordering the needed lab work, she decided she'd better check on Pop to make sure he didn't need anything. She wasn't surprised to find Scott in his room. Pop was awake now, and showed none of the signs of fatigue and confusion she had seen earlier. Moving into the room, she noticed a younger man standing by.

"I don't understand, Pop—why did you leave the house without calling me? I could have brought you to the hospital if you weren't feeling good," the young man said, and then turned toward her and Scott. "Is he okay? He has some problems with his heart, but the doctor said all his tests were good at his last visit."

"Hi, I'm Lacey," she said. "Are you related to Mr. Myers?"

"This is his son, Jack," Scott said. "He lives with his father."

Lacey was impressed with how fast Scott had been able to locate Pop's family—but then he was Scott. The man had a ridiculous amount of contacts in the city. If Scott didn't know someone who could help someone, he knew someone who knew someone who could. It was why his local veterans' program was doing so well. He had the will and the contacts needed to make a success of it.

"Jack, your father came here to see your mother. He says she works here, but we haven't been able to find anyone by her name."

Jack winced as if she had struck him.

She watched as he took in a deep breath, then bent down in front of his father.

"Daddy, Momma passed last year. We went by the cemetery last Sunday after church—remember?"

The pain in the room was almost palpable. She knew first-hand that while grief would fade it never disappeared, and she could see the moment Pop comprehended what his son had said. The heartbreak in this elderly man's eyes touched her so much that she found herself wiping away the tears that had gathered unexpectedly in her own eyes.

As the son hugged his father he looked up at her and Scott with searching eyes. And when Pop had calmed down, Jack asked to speak with Scott. The two of them walked out, leaving her and Pop alone in the room.

What could she say that would help him? While she knew now that the man had lost his wife several months ago, to someone with the memory problems he was having it had to feel just like it had when he had first been told of his wife's death. She couldn't imagine having to live through hearing about Ben's death over and over. She had to say more than the sometimes scripted-sounding *I'm sorry for your loss.*

Kneeling down by the man, as his son had done earlier, she took his hands into hers. "Mr. Myers, I didn't know your wife, but I'd like to hear about her if you feel like talking," she said.

Talking about Ben with Scott and with her counselor had helped her deal with her loss. Maybe it would help this man too.

After a moment, with a faint smile on his lips, he began to tell her all about his Janie and the life they had built together.

Scott watched as Jack Myers escorted his father out of the ER. He'd had a long talk with the younger Mr. Myers and had recommended a local doctor who worked with dementia patients. While his father had not officially been diagnosed with the disease, Jack had known for a while that his father was having short-term memory problems. But, as most children were apt to do, he had been blaming his father's behavior on his age.

"Were you able to help Mr. Myers's son?" Lacey asked as she came up beside him.

"I gave him the name of a doctor to follow up with. And there are some medications that can help his father at this stage. He apparently started deteriorating after his wife's death. He cut himself off from his friends soon after that. He hasn't even been playing the piano since her death, which is something that has really surprised his son. Pop's been playing since he was a young kid."

"He's suffering from depression as well as the dementia," Lacey said.

Scott wasn't surprised that Lacey had

picked up on that fact. She'd suffered from depression herself after Ben's death, and had cut herself off from her friends and family before he had made it back to the States and forced his way back into her life.

And now the two of them were back at square one in their relationship. Even so, as hard as it was for him to admit, while part of him wanted to forget the kiss between the two of them had ever happened, there was another part of him that couldn't forget the pleasure of holding Lacey in his arms. It wasn't something he was proud of, but it was something he needed to face if he was going to be able to set things straight between the two of them.

"It's almost as if it's better for his mind when he forgets that his wife is gone," Lacey said.

"Yeah, that's what his son said," Scott said. "I also put him in contact with a friend of mine, to set up a time for Pop to go play at his club. Jack's going to bring him around and see if maybe that will lift his dad's spirits. I think getting him back out in the clubs is just what he needs. They were setting a date when I left them on the phone. You want to come if you're off? You connected with Pop and I'm sure he'd love to see you again."

"He might not even recognize me." She started to walk away from him, then turned back. "Do you really think it'd help if I was there?"

"I do," he said.

"And he's really that good?" she asked.

"One of the best," Scott said, then smiled.

"I'll let you know," she said as she walked away.

He knew she had a weakness for elderly gentlemen. She wouldn't be able to stop herself from wanting to be there to support Pop.

Scott looked around the unit after Lacey had left to deal with the next patient.

They'd held a normal conversation for almost five minutes. Maybe they could put the kiss they'd shared behind them. Maybe a night out was what they needed. A night away from everyone, where they could relax back into the relationship that they were both comfortable with.

But as he watched the redhead bend over a computer screen as she helped one of the newer nurses on the unit, he wondered if that was really what he wanted.

Lacey smoothed down her dress as she waited for the doorbell to ring. Nerves skittered down her back as she told herself once more that this was just Scott. She had no reason to be worried about tonight. It wasn't the first time they'd been out to listen to a live jazz or blues band.

Only this time it felt different—and it wasn't just the fact that she had taken the time to dress up in her favorite strapless dress and a pair of killer shoes that she knew made her legs look great.

It was entirely that kiss's fault. But it was totally ridiculous, and she had to stop letting that one small moment in time mess up her life. She'd liked how things were before they'd crossed that line from friends to…to something more. The two of them needed to discuss things between them like adults, instead of letting things continue the way they were now, and tonight, while they were away from the hospital and out of earshot of Alston, would be the perfect time.

The doorbell rang and, as usual, Alston beat a path to get the door.

Standing up to greet Scott, Lacey suddenly felt as if she was waiting for her prom date. Blowing out a breath, she made herself head toward the door after giving the babysitter some last-minute instructions. She knew Alston would try to wait up for her, but he needed to get to bed for school the next day.

She stopped as she rounded the corner and caught site of Scott. Standing there in a simple chambray button-down and dark navy dress pants, the man was a romance novel hero come to life.

There had always been competition between him and Ben, with the two of them arguing about who was the tallest, but height was the only thing the two of them had had in common as far as looks were concerned. Ben had been the dark and dangerous type—something that had pulled her to him—while Scott, with his blond curls and light green-gray eyes, had looked more like a beach bum than a doctor.

"Ready?" Scott asked as he smiled at her. "Alston says he's got the hottest babysitter on the block tonight."

She watched as a blush stained her son's face—one of the many things he had inherited from her when he'd gotten her red hair.

"You're not supposed to tell my mom

things like that. It's in the man code," her son said, then ran back to the living room where said babysitter was waiting.

"Sorry, I forgot," Scott called after him, then looked at her and winked.

"Man code?" she asked. "Why hasn't someone shared this with me? I might need to see this code before you start teaching it to my son."

Lacey let herself relax into the laughter they shared on the way to Scott's car, and to her relief the conversation between them remained on Alston's soccer schedule and Scott's work with the next Extreme Warrior challenge.

Arriving at the bar, which was named Jazzy Blues, after both types of music that could be found there, Lacey was surprised to see how many people were out on a week night.

It was easy to see that the bar had seen very little renovation in the last few years, with its scuffed-up wooden floors and whitewashed old wooden planked walls.

The bar itself ran the length of the room, and a small corner stage was set into the back of the room. In the middle of the stage sat an old piano, and she saw that Jack and his father had been seated next to it.

Making a path through the crowd, she headed toward the two of them.

"Wow," she said to Scott as the two of them wound their way through, "I didn't expect to see so many people here."

"I suspect the owner, Ronnie, has told a few people that Pop is going to be here tonight," Scott said.

He had moved closer to her so that she could hear him, which put his mouth dangerously close to her ear and neck. She felt a shiver run through her. Then the movement of the crowd, as someone next to her pushed their way to the bar, pushed her back against him.

His arms came up around her, to steady her, and suddenly her knees felt weak. She paused for a second as another man passed in front of her. The feel of Scott's body against hers was tantalizing. Then, taking in a breath, she forced down her body's irritating reaction and made herself continue toward the back of the room.

She had been hoping that tonight they'd be able to slide back into their comfortable friendship, but if she couldn't get control of herself the evening would be a failure.

Finally reaching the table, they took the two seats beside the Myerses. Pop Myers sat with his hands resting on the table, looking around the room. Would the man even recognize them or should she introduce herself to him again?

"Pop, do you remember Scott and Lacey? We met them at the hospital last week," Jack said.

His father smiled at her and Scott, then went back to studying the room. She watched as the younger Mr. Myers drummed his fingers against the table, then reached for the empty glass that sat on the table. Putting the glass back down, Jack laughed.

"I don't know why I'm so nervous," Jack said.

"Don't feel bad. I'm nervous too," Scott said.

He looked from the son to the father. Had he done the right thing, recommending that Jack got his father back into the world of music? He knew he sometimes had a tendency to get carried away with his wanting to help others, but it had seemed such a simple thing to get Pop back out in the music community he had enjoyed for over fifty years.

The last thing he wanted, though, was for Pop or his son to feel pressured by something he had put in place. And it didn't help that he had brought Lacey there too.

He had thought it would be good to have her there, to give Pop and Jack the support they might need, but he hadn't known she was going to wear that sexy-as-hell dress tonight. And why did it bother him? He'd seen her in that same dress just a couple months ago, at a local art benefit, and it hadn't affected him the way it did tonight. He'd planned for the two of them to share a nice night out as friends, listening to some live music as they had dozens of times before. He needed to be thinking "friend" thoughts, not "boyfriend" thoughts.

"We never had this kind of crowd back when I played here," Pop said, startling all of them.

"You've played at Jazzy Blues before?" Scott asked.

They all waited while Pop seemed to be considering this.

"No, not Jazzy Blues… It was Norma's then, but it looks the same," Pop said. "But Norma never had this crowd. There must be someone special here tonight."

Scott wondered if they should tell him that *he* was the special person everyone had come to hear. Probably not, since that might be something that could upset the man. They didn't know for sure if he would want to play for them. Scott was only hoping he was right in assuming that since music had been such a big part of the man's life he would still be able to.

Scott recognized the owner, Ronnie, as he walked up onto the stage and a small trio, made up of a guitar player, a drummer and a sax player, followed him. Scott felt as nervous as he had once when he'd been staring down from the edge of one of Alaska's tallest mountains. He'd asked Ronnie not to make a big deal of Pop being there tonight, but apparently what he thought was a big deal wasn't to Ronnie.

Taking the mike, Ronnie welcomed his audience, and introduced the band members one at a time. "We also have a very special guest here tonight," Ronnie said, "Please join me and recognize the great Pop Myers!"

Scott watched Pop's face as Ronnie called his name. The elderly man had turned toward the rest of the audience when they'd started clapping.

"These people came to see me?" Pop asked, but his face was still calm, no sign of the panic Scott had seen when he'd been lost at the hospital. "Well, isn't that nice of them."

To Scott's surprise, Pop stood and headed toward the stage.

"Pop? You okay?" Jack said, and the panic that Scott had expected to see in the father's face was now on the son's.

His father waved at him, then went to the piano. The tension at their table increased as Pop studied it for what seemed like a long time before he struck the first chord and began to play.

The sweet sound of blues filled the room, and soon the band began to follow the piano player's lead as the crowd of people called out encouragement.

"I didn't think he'd ever play again,"

Jack said, then turned toward Scott. "Thank you. It means a lot to see him up there, happy again."

Scott gave the young man's shoulder a squeeze, and then let the music relax him.

"I have to say I had my doubts," Lacey said. She leaned over toward him and her auburn curls fell between them.

He felt an undeniable urge to reach up and brush them back over her shoulder, but knew he couldn't. Their relationship was fragile right now, and he didn't want to send her running from him. He wanted to deny the attraction he felt for his former best friend's wife, but it was getting harder to do that every day.

Was it just the kiss that had changed things between the two of them? Or was it that he was only now acknowledging that he felt more?

Realizing she was still talking, he leaned further over so that he could hear her above the band.

"It's amazing that this is the same man

we saw in our ER. He hasn't missed a beat and the crowd loves him," she said, as she swung her head around to look at them.

He caught a whiff of the perfume she wore. He recognized it as the scent she wore when she was dressed up, like tonight, and remembered that she had mentioned it was Ben's favorite. And she wore Ben's favorite perfume because she had been Ben's wife.

Pushing himself back from the table, he motioned to Lacey that he was going to get drinks. He didn't even have to ask her what she wanted; like many things concerning Lacey, he'd memorized her favorite drink years ago.

Scott stopped in front of Lacey's house and got out. While he had bought a loft apartment in the warehouse district, Lacey and Ben had purchased in a new gated subdivision north of the garden district, which had been built after Katrina.

Lacey gave him a speculative look as he

came around the corner of the car to the sidewalk that led to her front door. "You don't have to get out," she said. "Aren't you working the first shift in the morning?"

He wasn't surprised that she was nervous about having him walk her to the door. Hell, he was nervous himself after *The Incident*, as he had come to call it. Calling it *The Kiss* had brought thoughts of Sleeping Beauty, and he knew he was no Prince Charming.

Princes didn't kiss their dead friends' wives.

"Your babysitter forgot to turn the light on for you," he said as he pointed toward the front porch. "I'm just going to make sure you get into the house okay."

"I'm not helpless, you know," she said, then turned on her heels and headed to the door almost at a run.

He started to tell her to slow down before she broke her ankle, but the view she was providing for him from the rear took his speech away.

Nope, he was definitely no prince.

She punched a code into her front door and then, breathless, turned back toward him. He could understand why Lacey had been a bit skittish these last few days, but he was starting to wonder if maybe it was more than just the fact that he had kissed her. Was there something else that was bothering her?

"I'm so glad I got to go tonight. Pop was amazing on the piano and I think it helped him to be out there. Did you see the smile on his face when he finished the set and everyone was clapping?" she said.

"I think he enjoyed the attention as well as the playing, but we both know that tomorrow he might not remember that he even played there tonight," Scott said.

"I know… But Jack said the doctor you recommended has started his dad on new medication, and he seemed very hopeful.

The owner of the club was talking to Jack about having Pop perform again."

Scott felt the awkwardness between them as they stood at the door. He felt like a teenager, working up the courage to go in for his first kiss.

That thought sent him scurrying back off the porch. Now who was the skittish one?

"It was a good night," he said as he started backing away from the house. "Goodnight," he called.

He headed back to his car. Then sat in his seat for a moment after Lacey had shut her door. It was as if that one kiss they'd shared had turned on some sex-starved gene in his body and now he found himself acting like a fool every time he was alone with her. And that was not going to be tolerated. Either they worked this thing out between the two of them or...

Or what? That was the problem. He wasn't certain how they could work things out without them going either one way, in which he returned to the comfortable relationship of being her late husband's best friend, or another way, in which they moved on to something else. Something more than friends?

Shaking his head at that prospect, he turned his ignition on and headed for home, where he knew he would spend another sleepless night.

CHAPTER FOUR

SCOTT HUNG UP the phone and checked off the last number he had on the roster of volunteers who helped with events on his Extreme Warrior program.

When John, one of the nurses who had signed up to help with the swamp hike, had been called out of town with a family emergency, Scott had never thought he wouldn't be able to find a replacement for him, but it looked as if every volunteer he had was either out of town or already working.

The only person left for him to call for help was Lacey.

Up to this point the only work Lacey had done with the program had been to help with the registration and the running of the marathon they held every year in the city, with the proceeds going to help with the funding of the program. She'd always shied away from being involved in the more extreme challenges the group of veterans took part in.

She had never been able to understand why he and the others felt the need to climb the tallest mountain or shoot the most dangerous rapids. He'd tried to explain to her that he and the other veterans felt a need to prove to themselves—and, yes to others too—that they could still do all the things they'd been able to do before they had been injured, as well as things they had never dreamed of being able to do even before their injuries.

And then there was the issue they were having with being comfortable around each other now.

Things between the two of them were complicated, but he still felt sure Lacey wouldn't let him down. And, while Lacey had never claimed to be a fitness junkie, hiking some of the swamps in Louisiana was a very tame trip compared to most of the events the program sponsored.

He decided it would be better if he texted her instead of having to grovel on the phone. If he couldn't get another volunteer, another nurse to go with him, he would have to cancel the hike, and he didn't want to disappoint all the vets who had been planning for and looking forward to the hike for weeks.

Pulling out his phone, he began to type.

Hey, I've got a problem and I need some help.

He waited a moment to see if she would respond. There was the possibility that she was working and wouldn't be able to get back to him right away.

Then she texted back.

Okay. What do you need?

There's a little problem with the hike this weekend.

What kind of problem?

I need a volunteer to go with me. John had a family emergency and had to cancel.

He waited a minute. There was no sign that she was typing. If she couldn't do it he would just have to cancel. He couldn't take a bunch of beginners out without the help he would need if something happened.

Finally she texted back.

The hike in the swamp? Where there are mosquitos as big as herons and nasty water filled with snakes and gators? Do you realize how many germs there are out there in that water?

He couldn't help but laugh.

Yes, that's the one. I promise I'll protect

you from any gator that decides to get frisky with you.

The gators get frisky? Nope, sorry. I am not having any part of frisky gators.

Come on, Lacey. I've called all the other volunteers and I really need a nurse beside me, just in case something goes wrong.

Yeah, it's the something going wrong with the gators that I'm worried about.

He waited for a minute. Lacey knew most of the vets on the program and he didn't believe she would let them down.

She typed back.

Did you ask Sarah?

Grandkid's birthday.

Ryan?

I've asked everyone. You're the only one who isn't either out of town or working. You're not working, are you?

No…

Alston can stay with my mom for the weekend. I'll get my sister to pick him up from school Friday. He'll love it.

He waited. No response.

Please?

She sent him a series of expressive emojis that he knew implied that she wasn't happy.

Okay, but there'd better not be any frisky gators within twenty yards of me at any time.

Ten yards…?

He laughed when she sent him an extremely rude emoji, then put his phone down and went back to his maps.

If Lacey was going to agree to come with them he'd have to do something about the second part of the trail he had planned to take. Nothing extreme…just something special that she would be sure to enjoy.

Lacey parked her car. She'd wanted to call in sick today, but how did you call in sick if you were a volunteer? Not that she'd really volunteered for this… But Scott asked so little of her that she couldn't turn him down.

Since Ben's death he'd been there whenever she had needed him. Though Scott had been in the hospital long after the explosion had killed Ben, he'd still called her every night just to see how she and Alston were holding up. And after Scott had finished rehab he'd been over to their house at least once a week, helping her with the chores that normally Ben would have done.

She had started to remind him that she had handled everything by herself before, when Ben was deployed, but she'd been able to see that it had helped him to feel that he was needed so she'd accepted his help.

He'd even driven her to her grief counselor the first time, and when the counselor had recommended doing yoga he'd taken a couple of classes with her. She still had a couple photos of him trying to do the Downward Dog that she had kept for blackmail purposes.

Scott had also been there the day she'd decided it was time to pack up Ben's closet. He'd held her as she had broken down over and over again that day. He'd even broken down with her at one point. He'd been there and he'd understood what she was going through because he had loved Ben too.

It was all those things that they had shared for those first few months that had bonded them together as friends. And now she could feel that things were changing between the two of them and she was afraid of where that change would lead them.

A knock on her car window brought her back to the present. A woman she had seen at the last marathon stood by the door. Katie? Kathy?

Lacey got out of the car. It would be okay. If this woman who'd lost part of her arm could stand there with such excitement on her face at the prospect of hiking in the humid September heat, she could and would do this. She owed it to Scott and to the rest of the party to make the best of this situation and she would.

"Hello, nice shoes," the woman said as she looked down at the waterproof hiking boots Lacey was wearing—pink, covered in rubber duckies. "Scott asked me to keep a lookout for you. He seems to think you might bolt once you get here."

"Thanks—and, nope, I'm here to stay," Lacey said. "I'm Lacey."

"I'm Katie," the woman said as they started toward the group that was surrounding Scott's car.

Scott had talked about this hike while he

had been planning it, so she knew it had been organized for a small group, with a combination of beginners and some of the older hikers in mind. She moved into the group and listened as Scott explained that they were taking two cars up to the Chicot State Park, where they would start the first leg of their trip, and then they would move out into the more isolated part of the hike.

When he told them he had a bit of surprise for them on the second leg of the hike Lacey moaned. Knowing Scott, a surprise on a hike through a swamp could be anything.

Scott looked over at her and smiled. Seeing how happy he was that she was there almost made this whole crazy trip worth it.

What had gotten into her? It was as if ever since that kiss they'd shared everything between them had changed. Scott had smiled that same smile thousands of times before, but never had it made her feel so warm and gooey inside. This was not acceptable. They needed to sit down and talk things out together, though there was very little chance of that while they were surrounded by eight other people.

Scott divided the group, and Lacey hopped into the car being driven by one of the vets she had known for several years—Dennis, who was the oldest in the group, and had been injured years ago during the Gulf Wars.

Scott had met him when he'd started planning his very first trip and had been looking for someone to help coordinate transportation. Since Dennis had opened a tour company after leaving the military, he had been the perfect person to help out. Ever since then Dennis had been part of the program, lending help wherever he could.

They arrived at the park and everyone began loading their backpacks. Scott had told her he would provide everything she needed for the trip except for her personal items, so her pack was lighter than the rest of the group.

She saw Scott loading his pack and went to offer to help.

"Hey, you ready for this?" Scott asked her.

She watched him heft the heavy pack up onto his shoulders and was amazed that he could still stand upright under the weight.

"I am. Do you want me to carry some of that?" she asked. It didn't seem right that he had to carry her provisions as well as his own.

"I've got it for now. Dennis and Max are helping too," he said, then reached into the backseat of his car. "Here, I thought you might be able to use this."

He held out a long wooden stick. It was a walking stick, with a carving of a series of alligators, going from a small one and progressing down the stick to larger alligators, till it ended with the carving of a swamp, with one large gator rising out of the water.

"Wow. Nice stick," she said.

"I thought you'd like it," Scott said. "Now if one of those frisky gators decides to go after you, you can just pop it on the head."

"Thanks," she said.

The thought of live gators being anywhere near her made her head spin, but at least now she had something to protect herself with—though she wasn't sure just how much this stick was going to help.

They headed to the start of the hiking path and Lacey fell into step beside Scott. "So how far are we hiking today?"

"Only twenty miles today," he said, and then smiled at her.

"Only twenty?" she said.

Lacey had always considered herself in good shape—she'd even run a couple of marathons back when she was younger—but walking twenty miles in the Louisiana heat was not something she was looking forward too.

One of the vets pointed out a large heron that was feeding next to the path. Its long legs allowed it to stand in the water and look down into the murky depths as it searched for prey.

As they walked the group became quieter, as if in consensus that they would try not to disturb the peacefulness of the park.

Lacey found herself looking for gators as they traveled farther into the hike, and she stopped when she spotted a head sticking out of the water. She'd swear those beady eyes were looking right at her. She gripped the stick in her hand tighter. Just let one of those monsters come toward her. She'd show them who was at the top of the food chain.

"Do you need a break?" Scott asked, and laughed when she jumped.

Looking around, she noticed that she had fallen behind the other hikers.

"Sorry. I'm good. I just wasn't paying attention like I should have been."

She'd kept her eyes on that floating head, and noticed that it had sunk back under the water when Scott had arrived. She'd rather it had stayed up above the water, where she could watch it. Now it could be anywhere.

She picked up her pace so that she could catch up with the rest of the group. There was safety in numbers, she'd always heard.

"Whoa, you don't have to run. We're doing well with our time so far. We'll make it to the campground in plenty of time to set up camp," Scott said.

"Good," she said, as the path took a turn away from the swamp and into an area heavily populated with cypress trees.

Oh, great. Now instead of gators she had to worry about snakes.

When they'd caught up with the rest of the group Scott headed back to the front of the hikers and Lacey found herself beside Katie. They walked along the path with only the sounds of their steps and the sounds of nature surrounding them.

If it hadn't been for her fear of being eaten by an alligator or bitten by a snake, she would have seen how the beautiful surroundings could be peaceful and calming. She even found herself relaxing as the sounds of birds seemed to echo through the trees. A mockingbird started its complicated song, and she searched the trees trying to locate its position.

Katie stopped and pointed over to a log, where several turtles had hauled themselves out of the water and now sat sunning themselves. Lacey watched as one more turtle tried to crawl up the log and sent another one sliding off. The splash of the water almost covered the laugh Lacey hadn't been able to hold back.

She smiled as Katie turned around and they shared the moment. Lacey had always liked turtles. They were cute and mostly harmless. The world could use more of that, she figured.

After what seemed like hours had passed, Scott stopped and they all began pulling out water bottles and sandwiches. Scott had told her the camp they were staying at the first night would have provisions ready for them for the rest of the trip.

It was the rest of the trip that had her worried.

When their break was over they started down the path again, which seemed to wind itself back to the bayou. She continued to watch out for anything that could possibly eat her, but found herself relaxing when Scott fell back to walk with her. The miles started to stretch out as the afternoon heat began to cut through the coverage of trees.

Stopping to catch her breath, she motioned for Scott to continue without her. "Don't stop...save yourself. I'll just stay here and be gator bait," she said.

She pushed the wet tendrils of hair that had fallen out of her ponytail off her face. It wasn't that she was particularly a Barbie doll kind of girl, she just didn't see the need to go outside and do things that made you sweaty and stinky—both of which she was now.

"Come on, we only have another mile and a half to go," Scott said as he looked down at his phone. "You can make it."

Lacey took in a couple more deep breaths, then straightened up. She could do this.

As Scott headed back to the front of the group, so that he could show them the course to take toward the campsite, Katie dropped back with her.

"I'm sorry I'm slowing you down," Lacey said. "You don't have to wait for me."

"You're fine," Katie said. "I'm starting to get tired too."

"You don't look it. I'm sweating like a

wild pig," Lacey said. "You don't even seem winded."

Katie smiled at her. "You haven't had the training I've had. Besides, summers in Afghanistan were hot and dry. I prefer humidity."

"Wow. I've never heard anyone say they *like* the Louisiana humidity," Lacey said. "It must have been really bad over there, huh?"

"The temperature was bad, but that was definitely not the worst the place had to offer," Katie said.

Katie's face fell, and Lacey knew she was thinking of the fighting and loss of life she had seen. Katie's life had changed when she'd come back without her arm. Lacey's life had changed when Ben had been killed. They had both lost, but the two of them were still here, still fighting to make a life out of what they had left.

For the first time that day Lacey was glad she had come on the trip. While she had always helped Scott occasionally with the program, she had been careful not to get too involved with its members. She knew that there was a possibility that some of them might have known her husband, and she didn't know if she wanted to share the memories they had with Ben.

She had still been feeling vulnerable when Scott had launched the program, and she had still been carrying a lot of anger—not only for the man who had killed her husband, but also for the fact that her husband had been over there in the first place.

Ben hadn't been a soldier—he'd been a doctor.

When they'd first met at the local college Ben had talked of coming back to Louisiana after he'd finished his residency. It hadn't been until after they had started making plans for their future together that he had brought up going into officer training with the military.

Even after he had gotten her to agree with his plans she had never considered that he might die while serving his country. She had thought that, being a doctor, he would be far away from actual danger.

She had been so naïve. But Ben hadn't been. He would have had to know that he was at risk of being injured or worse while he was overseas, but he had never told her…never discussed the possibility of his not coming back.

Lacey saw a clearing up ahead and knew it was their camp ground when one of the other members let out a holler. Lacey dropped her pack where she stood and stared at the small buildings in front of her. They might not look like much to some people, and they definitely weren't five-star hotels, but they were a lot more shelter than she had hoped for on this trip.

Scott assigned the buildings—one for the men and one for the women—and they split up to stow their gear. They were all surprised to find a small bathroom inside the small bunkhouse, and they each took a turn at a cold shower before they headed back out.

By the time Lacey had showered and changed a fire had been built in the center of camp. An in-ground grill had been lit and a large amount of meat was grilling. She stopped by where Scott stood, beside a set of ice chests.

"Where did these come from?" she asked.

"I got one of the park rangers to bring them down from my car. We'll carry some of the bread for tomorrow night, but the rest we need to eat tonight." Scott said.

Lacey moved over to where Katie was wrapping potatoes and corn in foil. They worked together quickly, then agreed that they deserved a break after opening another cooler and finding it full of cold drinks.

As the hot sun set they gathered around the table to eat. And after everything was cleaned up around the campsite Lacey wandered over to the fire, where someone had found sticks for toasting marsh-mallows.

Lacey watched as Scott moved around the camp. His limp was more pronounced tonight—undoubtedly from the amount of time he had spent walking today. She knew that he still suffered pain due to his injury, though he tried to hide that fact from everyone. Watching his face, she saw the small grimace he made as he walked back over toward the fire.

"Come sit down beside me," she said.

"I didn't want to disturb you," he said as he sat on a tree stump next to her. "You've been quiet tonight. I figured you'd head to bed the first chance you got."

"I'll head that way soon," she said. "How are you doing?"

She had to be careful when asking Scott about his injury. He made every attempt to ignore it and she knew he wouldn't want her to be worried about him.

"Tired…but in a good way, you know?" he said.

"Yeah, I'm surprised to say that I can understand that," Lacey said.

She picked up one of the logs that had been left at the side of the fire and carefully placed it on top of the other burning wood. As they sat there in silence, with both of them staring into the fire, she wondered where Scott's thoughts were right then. Was he back remembering another time, before the world had changed, perhaps when he'd sat around a fire like this with his friends? With Ben? Or did the bright flames and the smell of burning wood take him back to Afghanistan? To the explosion that had injured his leg? That had killed Ben?

He'd never shared anything about what had happened that day and she had never asked. Some things she didn't need to know.

Looking around the campground, she was surprised to see they were the only two who hadn't headed into the cabins.

How long had they been sitting there, just the two of them?

She looked up to the sky and saw that there was only a small sliver of the moon shining through the clouds. She heard the hoot of an owl in the distance and heard the crackle of the fire as one of the logs broke apart into bright embers.

"I like this," Scott said.

"It's a nice area, and the cabins are definitely a bonus," Lacey said.

She reached for another log when she saw that the last one had already burned. Then she picked up one of the sticks they had used for the marshmallows and stirred the embers.

"No, I like sitting here with you," Scott said.

Lacey's hand froze. The stick in her hand began to burn and she tossed it into the fire. What was Scott saying? She felt that he wanted something more from her. More than the friendship they had shared. *Had* shared? No, they were still friends. It was just that they had complicated things between the two of them with feelings that they knew weren't right.

She wanted to beat her head against the ground till she figured out exactly what it was that was going on between the two of them, but she knew all she'd have was a headache and still no answers. She didn't want to have this conversation, but she knew that it was needed, so that they could return to the way things had been before they'd messed up.

"I enjoy being with you too, Scott," she said. "It's something that has always made our friendship special. I've never had to watch what I say or do with you. Being with you has always made me feel comfortable."

Scott knew without her saying anything more where she was headed with this conversation. She found their relationship *comfortable*. Like an old pair of shoes.

Was that what she had always thought of their relationship?

He made himself stop before he said something that would make things worse. And, really, could he blame her for the way she felt? Hadn't he felt the same? If he had never kissed her at the hospital would they be sitting here now, discussing relationships and feelings?

But had it only been the kiss that had changed things between them? If he was honest with himself—really honest—he had to admit that his feelings for Lacey over the past year had been changing. He'd even stopped dating after he had started to compare the last two girls he'd gone out with to Lacey. He'd told himself that he just needed a break from all the drama that came with dating, and that his life was full with his job and the vets he worked with on the program.

And with Lacey and Alston.

They'd been a big part of his life ever

since Ben had died, and at some point his time with Lacey had become less about helping Ben's widow and more about spending time with her. And that was something that was never supposed to happen and it wasn't something he was proud of.

He'd managed to put his attraction to Lacey away years ago, after Ben had come home one night and declared that Lacey was *the one* for him. And since the day he had stood as Ben's best man at their wedding he had looked at Lacey as his best friend's wife.

But how did he explain all this to Lacey without it coming out as if he was some jerk trying to hit on his best friend's wife?

"I'm not sure what to say to you," Scott said.

He always tried to be honest with people, and this was especially true with Lacey. He didn't want to lay out all his feelings for her, but he had to at least be honest.

"I'd like to say that I'm sorry I kissed you, that I crossed the line of friendship, but I can't. We both know that I...we were both upset that night, and maybe if I hadn't experienced that fear of losing you I wouldn't have kissed you. But I did. And you kissed me back."

"I didn't mean to," Lacey said.

He watched as she picked up another stick from the ground and began raking it across what was left of the fire.

She looked over at him and he couldn't help but smile. She'd pulled her hair back from her face, and even though he was sure she'd covered herself in sun protectant a scattering of freckles was now sprinkled across her face. Her eyes were bright green tonight, as the light from the embers in the fire reflected off them. He saw that she was working through what he had said.

"But you did. I can't lie to you and tell

you that I regret that, or that I'm sorry for kissing you in the first place. Whether it was fueled by the adrenaline of the night or it was something that would have happened eventually, I don't know. What I *do* know is that it was a wonderful kiss and every time I see you I think about it. And don't tell me you haven't thought about it too," he said.

"So where do we go from here?" she asked. She dropped the stick she'd been doodling with and looked up at him.

"I think that's up to the two of us," he said. "It could be that it was just a one-time fluke, and if we kiss again neither of us will feel a thing. Or it could be that there is an attraction between us that we are only just now discovering."

"And how do you suggest we find out which it is?" she asked. She was looking down at the ground now.

"There's really only one way to find out," he said.

Putting his hand under her chin, he

guided her eyes up to his. She stared back at him, then her expression changed. Her chin tilted up and her eyes filled with determination.

His lips touched hers for the briefest of moments and then she pulled away quickly.

"See—nothing. No fireworks, no angels singing. We're fine," she said.

Did she really think she was going to get away with that?

"That doesn't count. I've had longer kisses from my Aunt Jo," he said. "Now, are we going to do this right or are you too scared to find out the truth?"

"I'm not scared," she grumbled.

He watched as she stuck that same determined mask on her face again. "Okay, I'm ready."

He felt like a bull having a red flag waved before him.

The hell with it all.

He moved onto the log where she sat and took her face in both of his hands.

Impatience drove his lips down to hers, and before she had time to react he had pushed his hands into her hair. Tearing off her hairband, he caught the thick red mass in his hands. His lips pressed into hers and when she opened her mouth his tongue slid in.

He had no time to wait for her response. He'd spent days thinking of kissing her, and if this was his only chance he would enjoy every moment of it. He felt her hands come up between them and feared she would push him away. When she gripped his shirt and pulled him closer he would have sworn he heard those angels she'd mentioned singing.

His tongue tangled with hers and he felt the need to delve deeper, faster. His hand had found the hem of her shirt before he realized what he was doing. Cool skin filled his hand as it worked its way up her chest.

Lacey released his shirt and covered his hand. Pulling back from her, he was surprised to find that she was almost lying in his lap. He removed his hand from under her shirt and she moved away from him. Though neither of them could talk yet, Lacey's movement told him all he needed to know.

They sat there in silence as they both fought to fill their lungs with air, and then Lacey stood and walked away from him.

There was no way she could deny the attraction between the two of them, but that didn't mean she liked it. And could he blame her? They'd had a safe relationship, and they both knew that Lacey liked to play it safe.

The clouds cleared from the sky and the moon shone down through the trees, bathing the ground in a soft light. Bending over the log, he could now see what Lacey had been scratching into the ground.

Ben's name stared up at him accusingly.

He had to accept that his best friend, the love of Lacey's life, would always be there between them. She had been married to the best man he had ever known, and Scott would always just be Ben's best friend to her.

And did he really deserve to have it any other way?

CHAPTER FIVE

THE UNDER-STUFFED MATTRESS had very little to do with the fact that Lacey hadn't been able to sleep. If her mind had been muddled before the kiss they had shared last night, now it was totally scrambled.

She'd all but run after Scott had kissed her. Even now the thought of what they'd done and what she had thought about doing with Scott set her heart racing. She'd agreed to kiss him so that she could prove to him—and, yes, also to herself— that the kiss they'd shared before had just been brought on by the moment. She'd been confident that under other circumstances she'd feel nothing when they kissed. It was Scott, for heaven's sake, her husband's best friend; she couldn't have feelings or desires for him other than as a friend.

But, boy, had she been proved wrong. There was no way they could go back to being friends after what they had shared last night. Could they…?

Someone knocked on the cabin door, and let her know they were moving out in ten. She hurried to repack her backpack. The last thing she wanted was for Scott to come looking for her. She had a lot of things to think about today, and being near Scott would not help her understand what was going on between the two of them. She would try to keep her distance for as long as she could.

They headed back to the trail they had followed the day before, then cut away from the path after the first couple miles. They sloshed through swampy water and she was glad for her pink boots. Unlike the day before, Lacey's mind wasn't on the dangerous wildlife in the area. Now the only thing on her mind was what she was going to say to Scott the next time they were alone together.

"So how long have you and Scott been an item?" Katie asked her.

"Excuse me?" Lacey asked, not sure that she had heard the question correctly.

"You and Scott," Katie said. "How long have you been seeing each other?"

"It's not like that," Lacey said. "We're just friends."

"I'm pretty sure there's more than friendship there," Katie said, "but if you don't want to talk about it that's fine."

Lacey thought about that for a few minutes as the two of them walked together. The rest of the group was up ahead of them and she was pretty sure Katie could have kept up with them if she'd wanted to. Instead she had chosen to keep Lacey company. She felt sure that Katie wasn't fishing for information for the gossip mill. And maybe what she needed was someone out of this situation to talk to. Maybe Katie could see things differently.

"What makes you think there's more than friendship between me and Scott?" Lacey asked.

"Well, there was all the heavy breathing you were doing when you came in last night," Katie said.

The veteran gave her a bright smile.

"I'm sorry. I tried not to wake you," Lacey said. "Did I wake the others too?"

"Maybe, but they didn't say anything," Katie said.

Lacey thought about telling Katie that she had been running, then decided not to. The more she tried to explain, the guiltier it would make her look.

"What else?" Lacey asked, curious about what the woman thought she saw in them.

"Well, every few minutes Scott is turning around and looking at you," Katie said.

"He's just checking to make sure I'm keeping up. He'd be doing that no matter who was in the back," Lacey said.

"This is not that kind of look," Katie said. "Just watch him for a few minutes. You'll see."

Even more curious now, Lacey kept her eyes straight ahead, watching Scott as he talked to Dennis about something on the map, talked to the hikers behind him. He changed direction, with the rest of them following.

She was about to look away, to tell Katie that there was nothing there to see, when she saw Scott turn around. His eyes met hers and for a few seconds they were connected. She could feel the tension between the two of them. His eyes bored into hers, searching for something—but what? What was it that Scott really wanted from her? For her to admit that she was attracted to him physically? He'd proved that to both of them last night. But they both knew that their relationship had to stay platonic. Didn't they?

Unable to stand the intensity of his stare, Lacey broke the connection between the two of them. There was nothing more for her to give to their relationship. They had to agree to go back to being friends. Only friends, nothing more.

Lacey looked over at Katie. One look at her face and Lacey knew she had witnessed the exchange.

"Told you," Katie said.

They followed the rest of the group into thick forest. Tall old cypress trees with large trunks jutted out of murky water, and the farther they walked the deeper the water surrounding the trees became. A splash in the water ahead of them reminded Lacey that this was a good place for a gator to be hunting for food. And as the water became even deeper she began to worry about whether the waterproof hiking boots she wore were going to be high enough to keep her from getting wet.

They reached an opening in the trees and saw a large lake spread out in front of them.

"I wonder why we're stopping here," Katie said.

Lacey watched as Scott worked his way through the group until he'd made it back to the two of them.

"What's up?" she asked, glancing at him for a second, then making it a point to look away.

"Yeah, why are we stopping here?" Katie asked him.

Lacey turned at the sound of the hum of a boat engine in the distance. Scott turned with her and pointed to a small dot across the lake that seemed to be coming their way. As it got closer Lacey realized it was an air boat, headed towards them. Maybe it was her lucky day, and instead of hiking they were going to be riding the second part of the way.

Lacey and Katie moved closer to the shore as the boat came to a stop. Lacey had seen airboats before, but she'd never gotten up the nerve to ride on one as they were usually used for taking people out to see the gator population—something that she had no interest in seeing.

The driver killed the engine and removed his ear protection. He offered a hand out to Scott, then pulled him into a man hug. She watched as they shared several animated moments that seemed to include an unnecessary amount of slaps on the back. Finally turning back to the rest of them, Scott introduced the man as a cousin who lived farther up the lake, and explained that they were going to take the boat over to the far side, where there was a path that would take them farther into the swamp area.

No one seemed to notice her silence when the rest of the group all cheered at this change of course the trip was taking. She wasn't surprised. She'd decided a long time ago that the people who went on these types of hikes had to be at least partly crazy.

"And this is Lacey," Scott said to his cousin. "Lacey, this is Rene. He's my father's brother's oldest son. You've probably heard me talk about him."

"You're the one who hunts gators for a living," Lacey said. Scott wasn't the only one in his family who liked to take risks.

"Ah, *chérie*. That is me. As I'm sure my cousin has told you, I'm just a poor swamper, trying to make a living off the bayou."

By the look of the large boat he was driving, she had her doubts about the "poor" comment.

Rene offered her his hand and she carefully stepped into the boat, where she found herself seated next to Scott. Reaching over her, he buckled her seat belt—something that had never bothered her before, though now it felt intimate.

Since that first kiss everything had felt more sensual and now, after the kiss they had shared last night, the attraction between them had increased to the point that every time they touched desire ignited between the two of them.

As his hands fell back into his lap she was reminded of how she'd felt last night, when she'd found herself half lying over him. There was no explanation, no excuse for what she'd done. The memory of his lips consuming hers and his warm hand against her skin sent a hot flush through her body—something she didn't need in the hot Louisiana sun.

The boat started up and began skimming over the lake, its speed making her head spin.

"You okay?" Scott asked from beside her.

No, she wasn't okay. She was about to have to end a relationship that meant a lot to her. Over the past four years Scott had become one of her best friends. The fact that they had bonded as a result of the grief they both felt due to losing Ben had never made a difference until now. Changing the rules of their relationship was not an option.

She nodded her head, and then turned her attention to the scenery around them.

Scott helped the others disembark the boat and gather their equipment. He couldn't help but notice that Lacey had headed toward the front of the boat, where Dennis was helping. From the way Lacey had left him the night before, he'd known that she would pull away from him this morning, but that didn't stop it from hurting. But he told himself to be satisfied with the friendship that the two of them had enjoyed the last few years. It had been enough before. Surely they could find their way back to that comfortable relationship?

But the truth was he wasn't sure he *could* go back. He'd gotten a taste of Lacey now and he wanted more.

It was his own fault that he found himself in this situation. He'd known he was being stupid, taking the chance of losing Lacey altogether, but he'd always been willing to take a chance when the prize was worth it—and Lacey was worth it.

He'd lived life to the fullest since he'd been injured. Witnessing all the death and destruction of war had made him see that nothing in life was guaranteed. You couldn't just sit and wait for things to happen. You had to *make* them happen. There were amazing things out in the world to experience and he didn't have the time to waste.

Lacey herself called him a daredevil, because he was never afraid to take a leap of faith, not knowing what there was on the other side waiting for him. He'd taken a chance the night before, by kissing Lacey again, and it had been just like jumping off a bridge with a bungee cord attached to his legs. He always had faith that the rope was going to hold him, and while he was flying through the air he never doubted that he'd be okay.

But he and Ben had taken a chance, returning to a war zone, and he'd lost his best friend. Now there was a chance he'd lose Lacey too. He just had to keep the faith that things between him and Lacey would work out.

Leading the group from the lake and back into the soft marshy banks that connected the lake with the deeper swamp waters, Scott made it a point to keep an eye on the terrain. He'd given Lacey a hard time about the alligators in this area, but even he didn't want to be surprised by any of the large gators his cousin had warned him about earlier.

He heard a scream from the back of the hikers and turned around to find both Katie and Lacey standing with their backs together while Lacey beat at the ground with her walking stick.

"What happened?" he asked.

"Something bit me," Katie said.

"It was a snake—I saw it," Lacey said. "I think I hurt it."

"Did it bite you too?" Scott asked as he grabbed Lacey and held her still.

Her wide eyes darted back and forth across the ground.

"Lacey, answer me. Did anything bite you?"

"No. I don't think so," Lacey said. "We were walking, and then Katie screamed, and I saw the snake so I screamed too."

"What did it look like?" Scott asked.

"It was brown and real long," Katie said, then looked at Lacey.

"And it had a yellow tail," Lacey said.

"Stay here," he said to the two of them.

Picking up Lacey's walking stick from where she'd dropped it, he began to push through the plants and logs that covered the area. If they could identify the snake, they could make the decision on the type of anti-venom Katie would need more easily.

"Which way did it go?" Dennis asked as he caught up with Scott.

Lacey pointed to the rear of the group, and Dennis and some of the others began to comb the area.

Finding no sign of the snake, Scott turned around to examine Katie's leg—only to find Lacey already rolling up Katie's pants.

"I feel fine," Katie said, but Scott could see that she was paler than she had been a few minutes before. "I've got thick boots. It couldn't have bitten through the shoe."

Lacey pointed to the red area right above where Katie's pants met her boots.

Giving up on being able to find and identify the snake, Scott pulled out his phone and punched in the emergency number. Katie would need multiple vials of the anti-venom that the hospital kept frozen in their pharmacy for an emergency like this. Speaking to the dispatcher, he explained their situation and they discussed the closest spot to meet the chopper. Closing the phone, he was glad to see that Lacey and Dennis had spread out one of the sleeping bags on the ground and laid Katie down.

"How you doing?" Scott asked Katie.

Lacey had cut Katie's pants up the side

and he could see that her leg had begun to swell.

"It hurts bad, but I've felt worse," Katie said.

"You're going to be okay, Katie. I promise," Lacey said, then looked over at him with eyes that searched his for reassurance.

"We both promise," he said as he looked down at this young woman that had already lost so much. He wouldn't let her down. He'd get Katie to the hospital, where they were waiting with the antivenom she needed.

"Okay, I need a couple of your walking sticks. The longer the better," he said, beginning to come up with a plan.

Dennis carried over two sticks that measured at least five feet. They would work. Discussing what other items they had among them, it was decided that leaving Katie on the sleeping bag and inserting the sticks into the sides would work—if the stitching on the sleeping bag held up.

One of the younger veterans handed over some rope and explained that if they tied the ropes onto the sticks it would help to support Katie's weight.

As the rest of the group worked on the makeshift stretcher, Dennis and Scott studied the map and spoke with the helicopter pilot. A clear piece of land lay two miles to the west of them. They'd hike to that point, carrying Katie, and she'd be flown to the hospital all within the hour.

"I cleaned the site, but it's still swelling," Lacey said as they began the long walk to their point of contact. "She will be okay, won't she?"

"The hospital has anti-venom waiting for her. We just need to keep her calm and get her there." Scott said, knowing that he hadn't really answered her question.

They'd both made promises to Katie and they were both worrying that it might be a promise they wouldn't be able to keep.

The people carrying the stretcher would switch out every fifteen minutes, so that they didn't tire out and slow down progress. And as soon as the stretcher was declared safe by Dennis, they set out.

No one spoke in the group. Everyone understood that getting Katie to the anti-venom as quickly as possible could mean the difference between life and death.

As the group walked Scott was surprised to see that Lacey was keeping up with the stretcher that carried Katie. She'd gone into nurse mode now, and she probably wasn't even aware that she had increased her earlier speed and was now as fast as with the most experienced of the group.

They heard the helicopter before they got to the clearing. As Lacey took a moment to check Katie's pulse, Scott gave report to the crew as they unloaded the stretcher.

"You need to go with her. If the poison affects her respiratory system you might have to intubate her," Lacey said as Katie was strapped into the stretcher.

"I know. Are you going to be okay?" he asked.

"I'll be fine—just take care of Katie. Her pulse is up into the one-twenties and the swelling is up to her knee now. If she loses that leg…"

"She'll be fine," Scott said, then called the group together.

Lacey watched as the helicopter flew toward the city. Turning around, she was surprised to see that everyone was staring at her. Scott had been joking when he'd told them she and Dennis were in charge now, right? What did *she* know about leading a group like this?

"So, Dennis, which way do we go from here?" she asked.

Walking over to her, Dennis showed her the map and explained Scott's plan to take a detour along a path that would lead them back to the lake. He would call his cousin when he reached the hospital and make arrangements for them to be picked up there. Dennis estimated that they would make it back to the original trail in a couple of hours, and with the shortcut Scott had mapped out they'd soon be back at the river.

The walk back was somber, with none of the joking that had carried them through the trail earlier in the day. The group had lost its leader now. With all of them worried about their fellow veteran they had become disheartened and there wasn't any way for her to fix that.

Or was there?

Moving to the back of the group, she pulled out her phone and checked for service. Except for a couple texts to check on Alston, she'd not used her phone in the last two days. She typed a text to Scott and waited to see if it would get through to him. He soon texted back that Katie was responding well to the anti-venom. After getting that bit of good news, she texted him her plan and told him what she would need to make it work. Having put everything into place, she moved back up next to Dennis and let him know of the changes.

The whole lot of them were dragging by the time they made it to the bank, but in only minutes she spotted Scott's cousin's boat, headed toward them.

As they loaded onto the boat she received a text from Scott letting her know that everything was ready. It wouldn't be the same without Scott and Katie, of course, but that didn't mean that the rest of the group couldn't enjoy their last night together.

As they pulled onto the shore from where they'd started their trip across the lake, only hours earlier, Dennis explained the change of plan and they all started back to the camp ground. She wasn't surprised when a cheer went up.

While everyone else headed for the coolers that had been dropped off for them, Lacey called the hospital to check on Katie. The charge nurse on duty assured her that Katie was doing better and that the anti-venom was starting to do its job. If everything continued as it was going now there would be no danger of Katie having any permanent damage to her leg.

Lacey ended the call and shared the good news with the rest of the group.

Someone had unpacked the food and they all made sandwiches. A few complained that this was not *true* camping, but most were thrilled that they wouldn't be relaying on the dried food they'd brought with them.

Unlike the first night when the group had camped together, tonight they gathered as a group. Soon a fire was built, and as they watched the moon rise in the sky they became more subdued. This bunch of people had been through so much to get where they were today.

She watched as Zach, one of the new members of Scott's program, who'd hardly spoken for the first day of the hike, pulled up the leg of his pants and showed the guy next to him his below-the-knee prosthesis. Somehow, in just a short amount of time, this man who had been a stranger to them had been taken in by the others and now felt safe enough to share the most vulnerable part of his life.

Scott had made that possible. Their leader and her friend Scott could do miraculous things for other people. He'd been there for her when she'd been at her lowest and had never asked for anything from her until now. But now she was afraid that Scott wanted more than friendship between them, and she didn't know what to do about it.

As Lacey watched the last couple of hikers head into the cabin she realized she was sitting in the same spot where she and Scott had sat the night before. Had it only been one day since she'd shared that second life-changing kiss with him? Looking down, she saw some of the scribbling in the dirt she had done the night before, surprised to see that she could still make out her late husband's name.

She'd been so angry after Ben had been killed. She'd been angry at the people who had caused his death and angry at Ben for not sharing with her just how much of a dangerous situation he'd be in at the hospital where he'd served.

Then Scott had come home and he'd been there to listen to her, letting her work through her feelings and never judging her. The anger was gone now, and she was learning to live as a single mom. Her life was calm and safe. Until now.

It was as if with one kiss Scott had awakened something deep inside her that she'd thought had died with Ben, and then with the second kiss Scott had changed all the plans she had for her life. And she had no idea what she was going to do about it.

CHAPTER SIX

LACEY WATCHED AS her son ran off to join the crowd of kids gathered around a table stacked with birthday presents. She had done her best to avoid Scott for the last week, but standing in his mother's backyard at his nephew's birthday party she knew she wouldn't be able to avoid him today.

She'd tried her best to come up with a good excuse for not being able to take Alston to Jason's party, but then decided it wasn't fair to Alston to keep him from enjoying a day with his friends. While Lacey sometimes found Scott's large family overwhelming, Alston loved to attend their big family gatherings.

Scott's parents' yard was filled with activity this afternoon, with a group of teenagers playing football in one corner while the younger kids played in the large blow-up bouncy house that had been rented for the occasion.

Turning toward the group of adults, she had no trouble picking out Scott among the guests, and as if he had sensed her presence he turned at that moment and waved.

"Oh, Lacey," said a voice from behind her, "we are all so glad you could make it today."

Lacey turned to find Scott's mother coming across the yard, carrying a tray in each hand filled with glasses of various sizes.

"Let me help you, Mrs. Boudreaux," Lacey said as she took one of the trays.

"Lacey, I appreciate your momma teaching you such good manners, but you know we don't stand on formality here. And with you and Scott... Well, he didn't want me to say anything, but it would make me so happy if you could call me Mary," Scott's mother said. "Now, if you could just take those drinks over there, by Scott, I'll carry these over to the kids' table. Make sure everybody knows that I've added a little something to the adult drinks. We don't want to get the two mixed up."

Lacey watched as the woman stopped at the first group of kids she came to and started handing out glasses. She seemed extremely flustered today, which was not like her normal composed demeanor. Was Scott's mom okay? Maybe she should mention it to him.

Of course it could be that she'd just had a few too many sips of the "adult" drinks she had specially prepared!

Scott met her as she crossed the lawn and took the tray from her. "I didn't know if you were going to make it or not," he said.

"You know Alston would never miss Jason's party," Lacey said.

"I left a message asking if you wanted

to ride here with me, but you never re-turned my call. You barely talked to me Tuesday at work. And you've ignored my calls. Any other man would think that you were trying to avoid him," Scott said.

"Any other man?" she asked.

"My self-esteem is higher than most," he said, then winked at her.

And there it was. That little bit of mischief that pulled her in every time. No one could stay mad at this man for very long—not when he turned on that Southern charm of his.

By the time they arrived at the group of adults Lacey had relaxed. Things would be fine between the two of them. Scott was back to his normal self. They could be friends—just friends—and forget about the complicated attraction between the two of them They were adults. They both knew that a little bit of sexual desire was not enough to risk the end of a great friendship.

"Oh, Lacey, we are so glad you could

make it today. It seems like every time we have a family get-together you're working. We've missed you," said Rayanne as she gave Lacey a tight hug.

Lacey pulled back and looked at Scott's oldest sister. She'd always gotten along well with Scott's whole family, but except for holiday parties and Jason's birthday parties, she'd not attended any more intimate family get-togethers.

Rayanne gave her another gentle hug. "We are all *so* glad about you and Scott," the woman whispered in Lacey's ear.

What did she mean about her and Scott? Surely Scott hadn't told them about the kiss they'd shared? Maybe Scott's sister had been drinking out of the same cup his mother had been drinking from.

Lacey pulled back and looked into the woman's eyes. They were bright and clear, with no sign that she had been into her momma's "adult" beverages.

"Mom," Alston called as he ran up to

her. "Can I change and get in the pool? Scott's dad is out there."

Alston knew his mother's rules. Even though he was a good swimmer, she'd never let him swim in a pool without an adult present.

"Sure—just make sure you listen to Mr. Boudreaux," Lacey said.

"Scott? You want to swim with us?" Alston asked.

"I'll be there in a few minutes," Scott said.

"Alston is such a good kid. You know we all love that boy like he's one of our own," Rayanne said.

Lacey gave the group a smile. Unlike herself, Alston had always had the gift of making friends easily—just like his father.

"Scott was telling us about the hike y'all took last weekend," said Scott's youngest sister Leslie. "It sounds so romantic. The two of you out in the swamp, working together to save that vet…"

"There was nothing romantic about it," Lacey said, "Katie could have died out there. There's absolutely no room for romance when you're fighting to save someone's life."

"Well, surely you and Scott were able to find *some* time for romance?" Scott's sister said, with a smile and a wink that matched her brother's.

At that moment the pieces of the puzzle started to come together. The over-the-top welcome from his mother, the strange comments Rayanne had made… It all made sense now.

Scott's family had decided that she and Scott were an item. But why? After all these years of being friends, why would they suddenly think that the two of them were involved? Because they had gone together on a hike? They'd gone plenty of places together over the years, and the hike had been a planned event for the veterans, not a romantic tryst for the two of them. There was no reason for them to think things had changed between the two of them.

But things *had* changed. After they'd shared that last mind-blowing kiss everything had changed. But there was no way they could know about that. Unless…

Lacey felt the rush of blood to her face. What had Scott done? Did he think just because she had responded to his kiss that he was suddenly free to share this with his family? She'd have to straighten this out right now.

"Do you have a moment, Scott?" Lacey asked. She tried to sound casual, but that was hard to pull off when her face was glowing like Rudolph's nose. "I need to discuss something with you," she said.

Scott looked over at her, and then he looked down at his feet. The man was busted and he knew it. She'd kill him for this. There was no reason for him to have shared what had taken place between the two of them with his family—with anybody, period. *She'd* certainly not told anyone. She'd never share something that personal.

Taking Scott by the hand, she pulled him away from the rest of the group. From the look on Scott's face, her smile must be horrific. Good—let him fear for his life. If he'd shared the details of their kiss with anyone she'd kill him for sure.

Scott stared at Lacey's face. He had known he should warn her about his family, and he'd planned to do just that when they shared a ride over to his parents' house. But she had been avoiding him and he'd never gotten a chance to explain things to her.

He'd have some groveling to do now, but surely Lacey would understand why he'd done it?

"Is there something you want to tell me?" Lacey asked, once she'd pulled them inside the French doors to his parents' house.

He knew she was using her "mom voice"

on him. He recognized it immediately as the one his own mom had used on him and his sisters. It was that tone of voice that could make him feel guilty without even knowing what he was supposed to be guilty of. Only this time he knew exactly what he was guilty of.

It had seemed so innocent at the time. When his sister had come to him with concerns, saying that it wasn't healthy for him to be spending all his time with his dead friend's wife and child when, according to her and his mother, he should be focusing his time on finding his own wife and family, he hadn't known what to say. If he'd tried to explain the guilt he felt that Ben hadn't made it home, or his promise to his friend that he would look out for his friend's family, it would have just upset them more.

The two of them moved aside as one of his nieces headed out the door to the pool. They couldn't discuss this here.

Now he was the one who took her by

her hand and led her to the back of the house, to his old room. Shutting his door, he turned back to Lacey. Her eyes, usually full of humor, sparked with anger now. He'd have to explain everything fast, before she went off.

"Look, I'm sorry, but it started off very innocently. I didn't mean for you to find out, or to have to deal with my family. You know how they are—they're constantly trying to get in my business, especially my sisters. Living with four meddling females has never been easy."

One look at Lacey's face told him he wasn't helping matters. How was he going to get her to understand that it didn't matter? What did it matter what his family thought? But of course if it really didn't matter he wouldn't be in the spot he was now...

"I didn't mean for things to go this far," he said.

"You didn't mean for things to go this far? What did you think was going to happen? You just said that they're meddlers. Did you think that suddenly they'd leave you alone? That once they knew you'd kissed me and I had responded they would stay out of things?"

Scott stopped his pacing around the room. What was she talking about?

"Do you tell your family about every kiss you have with someone or is it just the mind-blowing ones you share?" she asked. "And I've been thinking about that. How do we even know that it was your kiss that made me respond? Isn't it more likely that the fact I haven't had sex in the past three years is the reason it affected me that way?" Lacey said, and then she stepped in front of him. "I could have re-sponded to any man the same way."

Scott was getting tired of listening to Lacey's excuses for their attraction. He knew in his heart that Lacey would never have responded to someone else like she had to him, and it was time he proved it to her.

Crossing to the door, he locked it. He didn't want anyone to interrupt them. This see-saw of emotions would end here. He'd leave her in no doubt about whom she would and wouldn't respond to.

Turning back to her, he walked over till only inches were between the two of them. "Is that what you really think or are you just too scared to admit that you liked me kissing you?" he asked.

She knew just as well as he did that this thing between the two of them wasn't a fluke. He just had to make her admit it, so that this argument could be set aside once and for all.

"I'm not scared," she said. "I just don't understand why you want to ruin a perfectly good relationship because of a couple kisses."

Taking her face in his hands, he slowly lowered his lips. "Do you want me to kiss you, Lacey?" he asked.

He felt the shiver that ran down her

body. He watched her eyes go soft, then close.

"Yes," she whispered.

He placed his lips lightly on hers and pulled her body into his arms. He fought back the urgent need to possess her that filled his body every time he held her close to him. Instead he swiped his lips softly across hers, coaxing her to open for him. Her lips opened and he slowly let his tongue dance with hers. He felt her relax in his arms.

Moving his arms up her back, he let himself caress her. His body tightened as her arms moved around him and they moved closer together. There was no space left between them now. They moved as one as they fit their bodies together, her breasts pressed against his chest, his erection cradled against her abdomen.

He'd been afraid to let her see just how much she affected him the other times they had kissed, afraid that he would scare her away, but today she would know exactly what she did to him and what he could do for her.

His hands cupped her bottom and brought her up against him. Their kisses were driving him crazy and they were not enough. Her body slid against him and they both moaned. Did she know what she was doing to him? Did she understand that this was more than just sexual attraction?

In one movement he picked her up and laid her on the bed, pinning her down with his body. He drew back from her. Her eyes, clouded with desire, opened slowly and stared back at him. He wanted to watch her face the first time he touched her. He moved beside her and turned her toward him. He pushed her shirt up, then moved his hand over her breast. He could feel the hard peak of her nipple through her bra.

"Could just any man do this to you, Lacey?" he asked as his other hand undid the button of her jeans. He slid his hand inside and felt her through her panties. She pushed against his hand and he knew he had her. "Could any man make you this turned on?"

He pressed his hand against her sex and watched as her eyes closed in pleasure. She was so responsive to him. *For* him. He knew what she needed—what they both needed—but with his family just outside he knew they couldn't make love. Frustration filled him and his body protested. He'd started something he couldn't finish and that hadn't been fair to Lacey.

He lowered his head to hers and kissed her deeply. Suddenly she took over the kiss, her tongue stroking his urgently with a desperation that drained him of all his good intentions. There was only one way this could end.

He moved his hand against her again and moaned. She was so wet and warm. This was going to kill him, but he couldn't stop himself.

He parted her and felt the hard bud of

her core against his fingers. He increased the friction as he kneaded it. She shook in his arms as the climax hit her and he smothered her moans with his mouth. His body was strung tight with a need he fought to suppress. If he died here, with his hand inside Lacey's jeans, his mother would kill him.

The thought of his mother helped to cool his body's demands.

Lacey lay in his arms, limp and satiated. Seeing her that way made dealing with the frustration of his own body worth it all. He needed a cold shower, but a dip in his parents' pool would have to do.

When Lacey opened her eyes he couldn't help but smile. Her lips were red with their kisses and she looked up to him with soft, welcoming eyes. He smiled again. Her smile faltered and then her lips began to tremble. Was she going to cry?

"I'm sorry," she said as she looked away.

Was that embarrassment? The two of them had always had a very open relationship. They'd shared their feelings and thoughts without any worry of judgment between the two of them. That wasn't going to change now.

"Lacey, you have nothing to be sorry about. I love the way you respond to me. I don't want you to ever be embarrassed by anything the two of us do together."

Lacey looked up at him. She still seemed unsure—something the Lacey he knew never felt— but there was some humor in her eyes now.

"I'm not embarrassed by that," she said. "It's just that you… I didn't… I mean you still haven't…"

She straightened her shoulders and looked into his eyes. Now, *this* was the Lacey he knew.

"You didn't get anything out of that. I should have done something to…ah… help," she said.

Scott broke out in laughter, and then choked when he heard his mother's voice calling down the hall.

"Scott? Lacey?"

Lacey covered his mouth with her hand and he nipped at it with his teeth.

"I told you—I saw them headed over across the street," his oldest sister said. "I think they were going to check out that old creek bed."

He had no doubt that Rayanne had seen the two of them walk into the house. He owed her a big favor for covering for him, and he had no doubt she was already figuring out what she was going to blackmail him out of.

"Shh… If your mother catches us in here I'm going to kill you. And don't think I've forgotten about the little oversharing that has caused this mess you've gotten us into," she said.

They heard the back door open and shut and both relaxed back onto the bed.

"Why in the world did you think you had to share what happened between the two of us with your family?" Lacey asked as she chewed on her bottom lip.

It was something he'd seen her do a thousand times and it had never bothered him before. Now all he could think about was those lips and all the things he wanted to do with them.

Knowing that thoughts like that were only going to make things worse, he moved away from Lacey and sat on the end of the bed.

"I didn't tell my family about kissing you," he said.

"If you didn't tell them then why are they acting so strange?" Lacey asked as she straightened her clothes and sat next to him.

He noticed that she'd moved a little farther away from him. Was she regretting what they'd done? Or was she finding the proximity of the two of them together and the bed as much of a temptation as he was?

"You know how my sisters are always trying to set me up with their friends, right?"

She nodded her head and moved into a cross-legged position, scooting a little farther away again.

"I got tired of all the harassment from the three of them, and then one day Rayanne—who seems to think the world of you, so don't take this personally—started on at me about dating one of her husband's cousins. She said the family was worried about me spending so much time with you and Alston instead of trying to find my own wife and family. I told her that we had plans for the weekend that she was trying to set me up. She made a comment, said that the two of us would make a nice couple and it was too bad we weren't taking our relationship a little more seriously. I saw the way out of having to deal with her matchmaking and worrying my mother so I took it."

"You took it?" Lacey said. "What does *that* mean?"

She was giving him that stern momma

stare again, and he felt the need to squirm. How did women *do* that?

"I just told her that she didn't know everything about my life and that maybe we *were* in a serious relationship."

Lacey shook her head at him, a look of pure disappointment on her face.

"Don't look at me that way. It worked like a charm. Not one of my sisters has tried to set me up in the last nine months. And my mom's not always calling to check up on me." He said. "It's been kind of like getting one of those 'get out of jail free' cards when you're playing that board game."

"Well, I hope you've enjoyed it— because the getting out free part has run out and now we have a mess to fix," Lacey said as she rose off the bed.

Panic hit him. If his sisters found out he'd been lying about his and Lacey's relationship they'd make his life hell. And the truth was Rayanne hadn't been totally wrong. He'd already realized that he enjoyed the time he spent with Lacey way more than time with any of the girls he had dated. He couldn't admit it to Lacey, but his feelings for her had changed months ago.

Scott had always found his friend's wife attractive, but the friendship between him and Lacey had been casual. He'd respected her nursing abilities as they'd worked together in the ER, but his real friendship had been with Ben. His friendship with Lacey had really only grown after Ben had passed. They'd both needed someone to talk to, and the sharing of their grief had been brutal for both of them.

It hadn't been until the past few months that he'd noticed their friendship was changing again. How Lacey hadn't seen the change he could not understand…

"Are you coming?" she asked, and then froze. "Although maybe it would be better if we went out separately."

Scott looked up at Lacey and grinned. He'd learned a few tricks as a result of living with his sisters. Women were always concerned about what other women thought of them. It was something he never had understood. Men just weren't built that way. They were who they were and they didn't care what their friends thought.

"You know Rayanne knows we were in this room alone, don't you? She's probably already told Amy and Leslie by now." He watched as she nibbled on that sexy bottom lip of hers again. "If we go out there and tell them that it's all been a mistake they'll never believe us. How could they? I mean, how is it going to look if we say we were just passing the time, making out, and then tell them that we're just friends?"

Lacey looked up at him, her eyes narrow and shooting darts. Maybe that last part had been a little overkill.

"So what you're saying is that I'll look like a slut if I walk out there and tell your sisters that I was just making out with their brother, but they've totally mistaken the nature of our relationship?" she said.

He decided it was a good time for him to get up. Rising, he moved over toward the door. A little distance between the two of them might be good right now.

"That's not what I meant," he said.

No one would ever think such a thing about Lacey and she knew it.

"I know what you meant. You've gotten yourself in a pickle with your family and now you're looking for a way out. If you want my help, just ask. I'm not one of your sisters."

"Okay, I need your help. But I don't expect you to lie to them. We could just act normal and let them draw their own conclusions," he said. "Please?" he asked.

"It's not like I've got much of a choice, is it?" she said as she moved beside him. "I guess we'll just have to hope they have the good manners not to say anything about where we've been, because if they do…"

She didn't have to finish the sentence. He already knew he owed her for keeping his sisters off his back.

CHAPTER SEVEN

LACEY SPENT THE rest of the day and early evening with Scott plastered to her side. She'd wanted to needle him in front of his sisters, but she'd decided against it. If Scott needed her to protect him against his sisters' constant matchmaking, she would do it. Not that he'd really given her much of a choice.

As they moved from group to group she wasn't surprised by the looks they received from his various family members. While everyone had always been nice to Lacey, now that they thought there was something between the two of them his family seemed to have opened their arms to receive her.

By the time she had rounded up Alston and got him into the car she was looking forward to the peaceful quiet of her own home. She could feel the eyes of everyone on her back as Scott walked her to her car.

"Make sure your mother knows what a good time I had," Lacey told Scott, then leaned in closer to him and whispered, "You know everyone is watching us, right?"

"They're waiting to see if I kiss you goodnight," Scott said as he moved in closer to her.

She looked into the back seat, where Alston was buckled in and had started a video.

"I hate to disappoint them," she said— and realized too late that Scott had taken her words wrong when he dipped his head towards hers.

His lips touched hers for a moment and then were gone, leaving her wishing for more.

"That should make them happy," Scott said as he smiled down at her.

She didn't understand what was happening between the two of them. No matter how she wished it wasn't true, Scott was proving her wrong about their attraction to each other. It wasn't something that was going to go away if they ignored it, but she was afraid if they let it run its course there would only be pieces of their friendship left to pick up.

Still, looking up at him now, she couldn't help but think of what she'd experienced with him earlier. Just the thought of his hands on her sent a hot blush rushing up her face.

She turned her face away from him, hoping that he wouldn't notice. He'd proved to her that it was her attraction to him that set her on fire. She would never have been able to let another man touch her like he had, and that scared her. She'd only experienced that depth of desire before with Ben, and that had been so long ago.

If only she could accept what Scott offered her, but it was too hard for her to make that next move in her life. Was she ready for a romantic relationship? She couldn't deny the desire she felt for Scott, but where would that lead them? Their friendship was so important to both of them, and adding more to the mix, even if it was just sex, could be dangerous.

"Lacey, are you okay?" Scott asked.

She realized he'd been talking to her but she couldn't remember a word.

"I'm sorry. I must be more tired than I thought," she said.

"Do you want me to drive you home? You didn't drink any of that stuff my mom made, did you?" he asked.

He'd moved back from her now and she bent to open the car door. She needed to get Alston home. She needed to get away from Scott. A warm bath and a glass of wine would help to relax her and clear her mind. She had to figure out where she and Scott went from tonight.

"I'm fine," she said as she climbed into the car and started it up.

"I wanted to ask you if you're busy Thursday night," he said. "Jack called me yesterday and invited us to Baby Blues. Pop's playing there and he wants us to come."

Baby Blues was one of the top blues and jazz places in the city. The fact that they had invited Pop to play was amazing, and she couldn't help but want to see him perform there.

"Are you taking my momma out on a date?" Alston asked from the backseat.

When was she going to learn to watch what she said in front of her son? It didn't matter how involved he was with something else, he seemed always to be listening to her conversations—something that had gotten her into trouble more than once.

"Would it bother you if I took your mother out on a date?" Scott asked as he leaned into the car to talk to her son.

She started to interrupt him. Her son loved Scott like a favorite uncle—which was really what Scott was to him. She didn't want to confuse him, which gave her another reason to slow down and be careful before her relationship with Scott went any further.

"If you marry my momma would that make me and Jason cousins?" her son asked.

The shock of her son's question took her breath away. No one had been talking about marriage. Where had he gotten that idea from?

"Why would you ask that?" Lacey's voice was a high-pitched squeak.

"How about we save that conversation till later? Your mother is looking a little sick right now," Scott said.

The smile he gave her took her breath away, except this time it had nothing to do with embarrassment.

"Go home, Lacey. You can tell me if you're free to go out on a *date*—" he turned his head toward Alston and winked at her son "—tomorrow at work."

Lacey put the car in Drive and pulled away, heading home to her hot bath and wine, all the while trying to make an inventory of her wine collection in her head. Because at some point in the afternoon she'd realized that Scott's family were *right* to worry about her and Scott's relationship.

Over the last few years Scott had taken Ben's place in her life everywhere except in her bedroom—and now she was considering letting him in there too. She was definitely going to need more than one glass of wine tonight.

Lacey sat next to Scott as they drove toward the club where Pop would be playing and wondered for the hundredth time why she hadn't canceled this "date" with Scott.

The ER had been busy all week, and she'd been too tired to take the time to discuss it with Scott—though she had taken the time to tell her son that she and Scott had gone out together many times, and calling their time out together by another word didn't mean that things were going to change between the three of them.

When her son had asked her again about marriage she had tried to explain to him that she didn't know if she would marry again. She'd never hidden from him the heartbreak she had gone through after his father had died.

She knew that in some ways her explanation to her son made her a coward, but unlike Scott she had never felt that was something she needed to overcome. Fear was a healthy emotion that kept you from doing stupid things that could get you hurt or killed, and there was no reason she should have to be embarrassed by it.

Scott was quiet while they drove into the warehouse district of the city, where some of the newer clubs and restaurants were located. They'd both dressed up tonight, and Scott wore a dark charcoal dress suit that showed off his wide shoulders and trim waist.

Unable to find anything in her closet that she'd felt appropriate, she'd made a quick trip the day before to one of the trendy shops in the French Quarter and bought a short cocktail dress in a dark emerald green. Putting it on tonight, she had felt like a princess, and she'd forced her embarrassed son to dance a waltz with her in the foyer before being picked up by one of their neighbors.

She'd had second thoughts about the dress while she'd waited for Scott. The short hem and the low cut of the dress were made for seduction, and she didn't want Scott to get the wrong impression.

Or did she?

She didn't even know her own mind. The memories of Scott's hands on her as he'd brought her to orgasm had played through her memory a thousand times now, and still she didn't know how she

felt about this newest change in their relationship.

She didn't like change. She liked a nice,
orderly life. But now it seemed everything
but orderly, with emotions she hadn't felt
in years flooding through her. And while
she went through this repeat of puberty
she had to make sure she didn't give Scott
any false hope of their relationship leading to something more serious.

Lacey would never want to hurt him, but
she had no plans of marrying again. And
even if she did, it certainly wouldn't be to
a man who was just like her husband—
a man that would put his life on the line
while he had a wife and son at home, worrying about him. No, she didn't need another thrill-seeker. It had only been a year
since she had been able to stop seeing her
grief counselor. She couldn't take the loss
of someone else she loved.

They pulled into the valet parking and
she caught herself playing with the ruffled
hem of the dress. She did feel like a prin-

cess tonight, and she couldn't decide if that was a good thing or a bad thing. Ben had called her the queen of his life, but she'd never understood why. She'd been an everyday wife and mother who'd spent her time washing socks and cleaning bathrooms when she hadn't been off working at her very unqueenly job of mopping up blood and dealing with drunks.

The doorman opened her car door and she stepped out into a gated courtyard glittering with fairy lights. With its big pots of blooming pink and purple flowers, the place resembled a magical garden.

Scott took her arm and they were ushered inside by the staff. Here, too, there were pots and hanging baskets overflowing with beautiful flowers.

The sound of piano music greeted them as they entered, but it didn't sound the same as the music they had heard that first night they had gone to hear Pop. This music didn't pull at her emotions like the blues she had experienced then.

This music was intended to be only part of the background of the magical room they entered. The real music would start when Pop took the stage.

They were taken to a table in a corner, where they would have a good view of the stage but still have some privacy from the rest of the room.

"I thought we would be sitting with Jack," she said, breaking the silence.

"Pop's sister and his nephew's family have come into town for the show. I'm sure we'll see them before the night is done," he said, as he took the wine list from the server and then passed it to her. Scott had always been more of a beer kind of man.

She'd always been happy to let Ben choose the wine when they were out. But after Ben had died she'd gone through the wine he had stored in the small butler pantry in their house rather quickly. Though it hadn't necessarily been a healthy way to research wine, she had learned what she liked and what she didn't.

She ordered something she thought Scott would like, then handed the list back to the server. This was ridiculous. If Scott hadn't called this a date, they'd both be enjoying the night. Now everything felt magical and beautiful, but not quite the same. Where was that comfortable way the two of them used to talk together about anything and everything?

"Relax," Scott said, and then looked down pointedly to where she was wringing the linen napkin between her hands.

She made her fingers let go of the napkin and smoothed it back in place on the table, then replaced the silverware she had moved. Why was she so nervous? Maybe because all she had thought about since that day at his parents' house was how much she wanted him?

Her hand knocked against a crystal glass, splashing water onto the table.

Scott reached over and took her hand,

then rested it in his palm. She took a deep breath and made her body relax. She was going to make a fool of herself if she didn't get her nerves under control.

The piano music stopped and she turned as Pop took the stage. Applause filled the room, then quieted as Pop began to play. The music he played was all blues, and it tugged at her heartstrings. A young woman took to the stage with him, and applause broke out again. When the woman started to sing Lacey began to understand the true magic of the blues.

Couples were taking to the dance floor, and when Scott rose and held his hand out to her she placed hers in his.

Lacey let the music carry her off into another world, where the blues had been born. She could see a room filled with smoke, where the smell of bourbon and whisky drowned out the smell of spicy dishes and sweat. A younger version of Pop sat at the piano, playing, and a woman told a story of love and loss that brought tears to Lacey's eyes.

"There's something magical about his music, isn't there?" she said as they swayed together in time with the song.

"I believe so. He has a special talent. There's no way to know how long he'll be able to continue to play, but Jack's going to help his father enjoy the rest of the time he has doing what he loves, and fortunately we get to enjoy it too."

She relaxed her body against Scott's and let the music guide her.

As soon as Pop had finished playing his first set Jack brought him around to see them. Jack once more thanked Scott for all his help before returning to their table, where Pop's sister was wiping her eyes with one of the linen napkins.

The soft piano music once more in the background soothed Lacey's nerves and she relaxed as they ate, finding it easy to fall back into the kind of friendly conversation they had come to enjoy with each other. The music and the wine were doing their job and, combined with good food and conversation, she had to say that for a first date, if they were counting it as one, it had been perfect.

They left the restaurant with Scott holding her hand, and she felt none of the tension that had filled her earlier in the night as they drove to her house.

She had prepared herself for Scott to kiss her goodnight at the door, but as they stepped onto the porch she admitted to herself that she didn't want the night to end. But it had been years since she had gone out on a first date, and she wasn't really sure what acceptable behavior was now. She didn't want Scott to think she was inviting him in for more than conversation…

"Would you like to come in?" she asked as she opened the door. She tried to make her words sound casual. "I can make some coffee if you'd like."

Turning around, she found that Scott

had moved closer. Without waiting for his answer she turned back and walked into the house. She felt his eyes on her body and she couldn't help but smile. Yeah, she knew she looked good in this dress. It had been worth every penny she'd paid for it.

He closed the door quietly behind them. Turning again, she admired him. He moved with a stride that reminded her of a large tiger, stalking its prey. The look in his eyes quickly told her *she* was the prey.

"Coffee?" she asked, and managed to slip through his arms right before he could have her pinned against the counter.

Moving around the kitchen, she started a pot of coffee. She'd thought he'd follow her, and was surprised to see him punching buttons on her entertainment center. He took his phone out and hit some more buttons, and a few moments later she heard the unmistakable voice of Louis Armstrong.

"Nice," she said as she moved over to

the couch. Sitting down, she straightened her dress.

"Yes, *very* nice," he said as he leaned against the mantel of the fireplace and stared at her. "Did you enjoy yourself to-night?" he asked.

"You know I did," she said. "Everything from the food to the service was perfect—and, of course, the music."

The song changed and she recognized the next song—"A Kiss to Build a Dream On"—as it filled the room.

She smiled as Scott took a seat beside her. "One of my favorites," she said.

"I know," Scott said, then moved in closer. "Face it, Lacey, you're a romantic."

"Me?" she said. "You're the one who picked the music."

She'd known this moment would come when she'd asked him in. She wanted Scott to kiss her, to hold her. She'd had only a small taste of what sex with Scott could be and she wanted more, even though she knew she might regret it tomorrow.

She moved into his arms, no longer willing to wait. His lips touched hers as Louis sang about his sweetheart's lips and a kiss that only she could give him. Lacey let herself melt into the music and into Scott's arms.

One kiss stretched into another as the songs changed again and again. Desire for more filled her. Scott had removed his coat when he'd come into the room and her hands unknotted his tie, then moved down his chest, unbuttoning his shirt. She felt his hand slide up her leg and under her dress. She'd dressed in stockings and garters tonight—something she had never done before.

Scott's mouth moved down her face, then he nipped at her earlobe. "You are driving me crazy," he whispered into her ear.

He let go of her, then turned her so that her legs were draped over his lap. He worked his hands up her thighs, unhooking each stocking and rolling them down inch by inch. Then he pulled her into his lap. The cold air cooled her warm flesh as he pushed the straps of her dress down, exposing her breasts.

She moaned as he cupped her breasts in his hands. She wiggled in his lap and his hands left her breasts and clamped on her hips. She fought back her need to move against him, but lost.

He moaned as she moved against the hard length of him. "Lacey, I can't take anymore. Either I leave now or I stay the night," he said as he looked into her eyes. "I don't want to pressure you. If you're not ready for this, tell me now."

Lacey tried to clear her sex-fogged mind. She knew what her body wanted. It had made it clear to both of them. But what did she want in her heart?

She wanted to feel alive again. She'd spent the last few years mourning not only her husband but the life she had planned to share with him. She wanted to feel desired as a woman. She wanted to make love and have a man make love to her. Was that too much to ask for?

No, it wasn't. She was tired of fighting this thing between her and Scott.

She searched for the guilt that she had known she would feel if ever she decided to take a man into her bed who wasn't Ben, but it wasn't there. She knew she would have to take this one step at a time, but she would take that first step tonight.

She climbed out of Scott's lap and saw the disappointment on his face.

"I want you Scott, but I don't want to hurt you. Something died inside me the day I lost Ben. You know that. You saw me at my worst. I can never go back to that place again. Before we go any further, I want to make sure you understand that this—" she held her arms out to her sides "—sex, is all I have to give you. And I'm not even sure I know how to do that anymore."

She waited, feeling foolish standing in front of Scott with half her clothes off, and then he stood and walked toward her, his face unreadable.

"Come…let me show you," he said as he held out his hand to her.

She gave him her hand and let him lead her into her bedroom—the one room in her house that she felt sure he had never entered.

She hadn't been kidding. She really couldn't remember how this was supposed to go. Scott stepped behind her and unzipped her dress, letting it fall to the floor. She'd lost her stockings in the living room, and the molded top of her dress hadn't allowed for a bra. Now she stood in only the lace of her panties and her garters. She felt awkward and self-conscious.

She wrapped her arms around herself as Scott turned her toward him. He ran his hands up her sides, then took her arms and wrapped them around his neck. Her breasts brushed against the fine blond hair of his chest, the friction causing her nipples to peak. Her body arched against his as he took her buttocks and ground himself against her as his lips found hers.

Her hands found his belt buckle and undid it. Then she tackled his pants button and zipper, pushing his pants down. She might not remember everything, but she was pretty sure more than just one of them needed to be undressed if this was going to work.

She moaned as Scott's lips traveled down her neck to her breast, then made him answer her moan with his own when she reached for him and found him already thick and hard. He walked her backwards to the bed, then gave her a playful push onto the mattress that had her laughing. Yes, she remembered this now.

She caught two handfuls of his curls when he bent to her, and she took his lips with hers as she pulled him down. She felt him between her legs, then froze as she tried to prepare herself for the pain she felt sure would follow. She needed him inside her so badly, but it had been so long…

"It's okay," Scott said softly into her ear. "Relax."

She forced herself to relax and open her thighs as Scott ran his hand up her leg. He parted her with his fingers, then inserted one finger slowly as another caressed her. She felt no pain as she relaxed her body and let the motion of Scott's fingers give her pleasure. His fingers continued to pump into her, before withdrawing to circle the nub of her core, and her body bowed up off the bed as the orgasm built and then crashed over her.

Her body felt boneless as Scott moved his hand up to caress her breast, but she still wanted more. She reached down between them and guided the length of him, relaxing as his hips moved against hers. She looked up as he slowly entered her, with small shallow thrusts that went deeper every time until he was seated inside her. His face was beautifully strong and he held himself with such control.

"Are you okay?" he asked between clenched lips.

He was fighting for control, and while she knew he was only trying to be careful for her sake, she wanted him to move.

"Yes," she said. "Now move."

She wrapped her legs around him, opening herself up so he could go deeper, then began to move against him.

His lips slammed into hers and he took control of their lovemaking as he pumped harder and deeper. Her body tightened for a second time, and this time she couldn't hold back the scream that escaped into his mouth as his own coarse moan joined hers in their climax.

Scott opened his eyes and found bright green eyes staring back at him. The night before had been more than he had ever dreamed he would have with Lacey. And, though he knew that she'd turn away from him this morning, he was thankful for the time he'd had with her.

"What do you want for breakfast? I'm starved," she said as she rolled away from him and moved off the bed.

She'd slept in the nude and he enjoyed the view as she moved away from him and went into the adjoining bathroom.

Scott stared after her. He felt as if he had entered some twilight zone. Where was the Lacey he knew? Not that he didn't like this one; she just wasn't the one he had been expecting this morning.

He got up and looked around for his clothes. Pulling on his wrinkled pants and shirt, he moved to where Lacey had left the bathroom door open. He could see her nervousness now, though she tried to hide it.

He leaned against the doorjamb and watched her brush her hair. She'd changed into a pair of pants and a tee shirt that declared her a magical unicorn nurse—which made absolutely no sense to him.

What did nursing and unicorns have to do with each other?

She'd always been a beautiful woman, with that deep red hair and those green eyes that had a magic all their own. He remembered the heat in those eyes at his first thrust inside her, and then, after they'd made love, the way they had blinked slowly up at him as he'd tucked her against him and told her to go to sleep.

He watched now as her eyes seemed to dance from the mirror where she stood and then back at him. Yes, she was nervous, but she hadn't run away from him. Not yet. And nerves were something he could deal with.

It was a place to start on how he hoped their relationship would go from here—because, no matter what Lacey said, he knew she had more to give to their relationship than just sex.

Last night hadn't been just about sex, even if she wanted to believe that. He understood her reservations about opening her heart to someone else after the loss of Ben. He was scared to share his own feelings with her too, feelings that he wasn't even comfortable with himself.

"We could go by my place and let me change and then we could go out for breakfast," he offered. "What time does Alston get back from his sleepover?"

Maybe she'd feel better if they were out in public. He didn't want to scare her off, but he wasn't going to settle for just one night with her. They both deserved more than that. He just had to figure out how to get Lacey to admit that was what she wanted too.

"If you keep that up you're not going to have any hair left to brush," he said as he watched her jerk the brush through her hair over and over.

"That sounds perfect," she said, then put the brush down and turned toward him, giving him a lopsided smile. She really was trying to act like nothing had happened the night before, but she just couldn't pull it off.

They stopped by his place and he left her while he changed clothes. He thought about taking a shower, but he still feared that Lacey would run the moment her brain connected the dots and she realized that everything between them had changed once more. Lacey was a woman who liked lists and detailed planning, and he knew his spending the night with her had not been anywhere in her plans.

As they got back into his car he caught himself humming one of the Louis Armstrong songs that he had played the night before. They had gone a lot farther than one kiss now. That first kiss had changed everything between them, and last night would change them even more, but there was no going back now.

Lacey walked into the ER, dragging her feet. Alston had been home with a stomach bug, and for the last twenty-four hours she had been cleaning up after him. Single motherhood was such a glamorous job. She'd always sworn she'd never be a single mom, but she'd realized soon after Alston had been born that was exactly what she'd become. With Ben deployed, she'd been a single mom a lot of the time.

But now she needed to put a smile on her face and take care of other people's children, because that was her job. She rolled back her aching shoulders and soldiered on. She'd make it through this twelve-hour shift and then she'd go home and crash.

She heard a commotion in the first trauma room she passed and rushed in to see if she could help. A man lay on the table as staff moved around the room, each with their own job to do. Stepping in, she grabbed a pair of gloves and helped the med techs remove his clothes.

"What do we have?" she asked as she tossed the torn and bloody clothes over into a corner as she peeled them off his body, while being careful not to move him any more than was necessary. She noted an open femur fracture as she worked her way up.

"Motorcycle and car collision," answered the nurse across the room.

"Do we know who he is?" she asked Tess, the charge nurse she was supposed to relieve.

"Not yet. Paramedics called it in just minutes before they arrived," Tess said.

She looked at the table where the man lay still. An endotracheal tube protruded out of his mouth and his blond hair was matted with blood, curled around a face that was covered in road rash and cuts.

Her hand went to her chest as her heart dropped a beat. She headed for the pile of dirty clothes she'd left in the corner and found the pair of jeans she had cut from the man, went through each pocket, finding nothing that would identify the man.

She looked back over to the trauma table and forced herself to think logically. Yes, there was some resemblance between the man and Scott, but this man's build was stocky, where Scott was lean, with more defined muscles.

She took a calming breath. This man wasn't Scott.

But it could have been.

Scott had told her earlier, when he'd called to check on Alston, that it was such a beautiful day outside he was planning on riding his motorcycle to work tonight.

An ice-cold shiver ran up her back. She'd lived with all the chances Scott had taken since he'd come home from Afghanistan. She'd worried every time he'd left the country, looking for the next big thrill, the next big mountain to climb, the next extreme hike across Alaska, the next extreme cave dive. She'd made him call her as soon as he'd finished his ice climbing challenge and she'd chewed her nails down to the quick while she'd waited for that phone call.

But that feeling as if her stomach had

been turned inside out and her heart ripped from her body, that feeling of total devastation that she'd had for just a moment, when she had realized that it could be Scott lying on that trauma table, was more than she could survive.

She understood why he and the other vets felt the need to prove themselves, but she had never wanted any part of that life.

She moved back as the staff pushed the patient over to get a CAT scan, then headed to the locker room to stow her bag.

A case of nerves struck her as her mind lingered on the thought that she could lose Scott just the way she had lost Ben. She'd had problems after she had lost Ben— not only with depression but with anxiety too. She'd been shattered and broken and barely able to take care of her son. She wouldn't do that to Alston again.

"Are you okay?" Scott asked as he came into the staff lounge. "Tess said you were looking a little pale. Did you catch Alston's stomach bug?"

Lacey looked up at the very man who was causing her such anxiety. How could she tell him that she'd suddenly realized she couldn't handle the chances he took? That she didn't want to lie awake at night and wait for the phone to ring and someone to tell her that he'd been killed climbing some rock somewhere, or drowned in some cave in the middle of nowhere?

She'd buried her head as deeply as possible, but she could still see that Scott had hopes of a future with her. How could she take a step toward a future with Scott when it was too much to ask that he take a step back from that cliff-edge he seemed always to be running toward? Would it be fair of her to ask him to give up something that meant so much to him? Would it fair to her to live with the hidden fear that she'd someday have to bury Scott just as she'd buried Ben?

It wouldn't be fair to either of them.

"Lacey?" he said. "If you're sick, go home. We're not really busy right now, and I'm sure someone will come in and cover for you."

Her gut churned, and she wondered if possibly all this worry *was* just a result of her feeling ill or of her lack of sleep. Maybe after some rest she'd be able to figure out what it was she really wanted and what she could actually live with.

"Yeah, I think I'll go. I'll let Tess know and she can turn things over to the relief charge."

She walked right by him without another word.

Until she figured out what she was going to do it was better that she stayed away from Scott as much as possible.

CHAPTER EIGHT

SCOTT TRIED HARD to keep his mind on the conversation around him. He had picked Lieutenant Hines up at his assisted living facility, knowing that the group of veterans who usually attended his monthly meetings would enjoy hearing about the World War Two veteran's experiences. Unfortunately his mind kept wandering away from the discussion in the room to the one he'd had with Lacey three days ago.

He'd called and checked on her the day after she'd left work early, and she'd assured him that she was feeling better, but then she'd turned down his invitation to go out the next day. She was pulling away from him again and he didn't have a clue why. The only thing left for him to do was to confront her.

He looked at his watch. If the meeting didn't go late tonight he'd stop by her house on his way home.

He turned as the door to the building they rented opened and the woman he'd just been worrying over walked in, followed by Katie. Everyone rushed to greet Katie, and then the conversation turned back to their visitor.

Scott moved over to where Lacey had taken a seat and sat beside her.

"Do you want to talk about it?" he asked.

He'd always been attuned to the changes in Lacey's moods and he had no doubt that she knew exactly what he was asking about.

"No," she said.

He waited for her to say more. Okay, so she didn't want to talk to him about what was bothering her. Still, she was talking to him, so it couldn't be too bad.

"I'm surprised to see you here. What did Katie do to get you to come?" he asked.

"She didn't do anything. I offered to bring her," she said.

He let that roll around in his mind for a minute. Lacey had always limited her involvement in the Extreme Warrior program to just helping with the fundraisers they held, until she'd gone with them on their hike through the swamp. He'd tried to get her more involved over the years but she'd always resisted. It more than surprised him that she was willing to attend a meeting now. Maybe being out with the vets in the woods had helped her see how much it meant to them to have a challenge.

Scott had turned a lot of the administration duties he'd previously handled over to Dennis these last few months, and as Dennis now went through the minutes from the meeting the month before he knew he had chosen well.

He opened up a discussion on the next

challenge they had planned, in Peru, and one of the younger vets brought up the possibility of volcano hiking in Hawaii the following year. Scott saw the incredulous look Lacey gave the young man when he began to name the different hiking trails on the islands.

"Don't worry. The volcanos aren't active," he said, and watched her relax back into her seat.

By the time Lieutenant Hines had finished answering more questions it was late and the group started to break up.

"There's just one more thing we need to discuss." Dennis raised his hand as some of the veterans groaned. "I know. This will just take a minute. I got a letter in the mail today that I want to share with everyone."

It was common that when members moved away they wrote back to their friends as a group, and everyone always enjoyed listening to Dennis reading the letters. Everyone took their seats again.

"This letter is from the City of New Orleans. I read it earlier, and it's about as dry as week-old bread." Everyone laughed at Dennis's corny attempt at humor. "Basically what it says is that our fearless leader, Scott, has gotten himself nominated for a Special Citizen award. He's been invited to attend an awards dinner two weeks from now, where they will announce the winner."

Shocked at this announcement, Scott sat up straight as the other veterans gave him a round of applause mixed in with some good-natured heckling. With all the good programs in the city, how had his gotten this type of recognition?

Most of the members came by to give him a pat on the back before they left, or in Katie's case a kiss on the cheek.

He headed to the back of the hall to lock up the back door, then turned around to find Lacey standing behind him.

"I thought you'd left already," he said.

He couldn't help but reach out and push

a tendril of hair off her face and behind her ear. He let his hand linger over the soft skin of her earlobe. He watched as she turned her face into his palm before pulling away from him.

"You love all this," she said, and she indicated the room, where posters of planned trips and pictures from past challenges hung.

"I enjoy being able to help other vets, and you know I enjoy the thrill of the challenges. What's wrong, Lacey? You've been distant all week and I think I deserve to know why," he said.

She walked away from him and headed to the far wall, where pictures of the very first challenge the veterans had gone on were shown. Next to those pictures hung a five by seven picture of Ben, dressed in his officer's uniform.

"Ben used to talk about the two of you starting up a program like this when you got out of the military," Lacey said as she ran her fingers across the edge of Ben's picture. "He would be so proud of what you've done here."

"I hope so," he said as he came to stand next to her.

"I'm proud of you too, and I would never want to come between you and this group of vets," she said, then paused.

"I can hear the 'but' coming," he said. He turned towards her and took her hands in his. "Tell me what's wrong. It can't be that bad. Tell me what's happened that has you upset."

He took her chin in his hands and turned her face up towards his. He dropped a kiss on the tip of her nose and then her forehead, then waited.

"The other day at work they brought in a trauma patient, victim of a motorcycle accident, and for a moment I thought it was you," she said.

She pulled away from him and turned her back.

"I don't understand. This has something

to do with work? I don't even remember a motorcycle wreck," he said.

She was going to walk away from him and he still didn't know why.

"It was right at shift-change. Just before you came on duty. And, no, this has nothing to do with work. It has to do with the fact that I looked down at that man and remembered you had told me you were going to ride your motorcycle to work that day. It could have been you. *You* could have been lying there on that stretcher, tubed and unresponsive. It was just more than I could take," she said. "I know it sounds stupid, but it doesn't change the fact that someday someone could come to my door and tell me that something bad has happened to you. Or you could go off on this volcano hiking—which sounds crazy—and fall in and burn to death."

"Or you could have someone slit your throat with a scalpel while you are innocently doing your job at the hospital," Scott said.

His gut twisted at the memory of that night in the ER. He could have lost her.

Lacey turned toward him, surprise written across her features. Yes, he could understand the fear she was feeling. He'd experienced that same fear. Except it hadn't been about some abstract possible situation. He'd witnessed the real thing as he'd watched her life or death about to be decided by a deranged drunk.

"We can work through this, Lacey," he said. "I know that losing Ben the way you did was brutal, but have you considered all the wives who have watched their husbands die slowly in front of their eyes as disease took them? How many times have we had to tell someone that their son or mother or wife has passed away unexpectedly?"

"I know in my head what you're saying is true, but that didn't stop me from panicking when I thought it was you lying on that stretcher. You *know* what I went through after I lost Ben. You *know* what a coward I am," she said as she turned back to him.

"You are not a coward," Scott said as he walked over to her.

Would she turn away from him now? Could he have lost her before she'd even given them a chance?

"Yes, I am—but I'm trying to do better. It's going to take some work, and I'm going to need you to be patient with me," Lacey said, and then she turned toward him and walked into his arms.

He closed his arms around her. She was giving the two of them a chance, and for now that was all he could ask.

"Katie is waiting for me. I promised to take her to the hospital tonight, so that she can thank everyone who took care of her," she said against his shoulder.

He made his arms relax around her. She wasn't running away from him. Not this time.

As she raised her face up to his he lowered his lips gently to hers. Just that small taste of her was enough to set his body on fire. He knew he had to let her go, and that he had to trust they would get through this together. He was asking her to face her fears and now he had to face his own as he watched Lacey walk out the door—because right now he didn't think he could face his life without her.

Lacey tucked the little girl under the blanket and nodded to the red-eyed woman who sat at her bedside. The poor woman had been fighting her daughter's fever for hours before she had brought her into the ER and she looked like she was going to drop.

She handed the woman the extra blanket she had brought into the room. "Her fever is down. Why don't you close your eyes for a few minutes? I'll be back as soon the lab work comes in," Lacey said.

The young mother gave her a tired smile, then wrapped the warm blanket around her and closed her eyes. Lacey shut the door as quietly as possible, then headed next door to help Scott with another patient.

She could hear arguing before she walked in the room. At first she wondered if she needed to get in the middle of the patient and her husband, but it quickly became apparent that neither of them meant anything with their constant nipping at each other.

"I can't believe this has happened," the elderly woman said as Lacey watched Scott close up the laceration on her forehead.

Fortunately for her, the CAT scan had been negative, so all she would need was a few stitches.

"It was that greedy cat. She's always winding around between your feet when you're in the kitchen," the patient's husband said. "I told you this was going to happen."

The man had been grouchy since his wife had been brought in by the emergency medical techs, and Lacey had been listening to the two of them bicker back and forth for the last half-hour.

"It wasn't the cat that made me fall down. It was you, scaring me to death when you came up behind me. What were you thinking? I don't understand where your mind goes sometimes. We've been married almost fifty years now and you still think it's funny to sneak up behind me and pinch my butt? When are you going to grow up?" the woman grumbled.

Lacey watched as Scott paused with his needle in the air. Hadn't he done the same thing just last night, while she had been turning steaks on the grill?

She fought the laughter that wanted to explode out of her. Would this be the two of them fifty years from now?

The laughter died inside her. What were the chances that they would still be together in forty years? She'd spent the last three years of her life accepting that she would grow old alone, but now here she was thinking of a future fifty years down the road with Scott...

He finished the last few stitches and then, before leaving the room, he gave her a look and a smile that told her he was thinking about the night before too. Was he thinking of a future for them?

They had avoided the subject of a long commitment, which she knew was for the best while she worked through her emotions concerning Scott's way of life and his need to chase the next thrill.

She'd let him pull her into the planning of the program's upcoming challenges, and he had taken the time to show her how they worked through all the possibilities of emergencies and the strategies they used to decrease the risk of their being errors and injuries.

But was it enough to calm her fears the next time he left her to go on one of his extreme challenges? Probably not. Besides, why did *she* have to be the only one dealing with her issues so they could make this happen? Shouldn't Scott make some changes too? Would he? Or, more importantly, could he?

He lived for the adventures he went on, and if she insisted he stopped going eventually he'd resent her for it, and that wasn't what she wanted.

She gave the woman some discharge instructions, then went back to check for the lab work on the little girl.

After pulling up the lab results she walked over to where Scott was staring at his computer screen. "The lab work all came back clear on the little girl in Room Twenty. She's sleeping now and her fever is down. Can I discharge her after her fluids are in?" she said.

She waited for Scott to respond. He seemed mesmerized by what he was reading on the computer screen.

"Scott?" she said.

She bent down lower, to see what it was that had made him zone out on her, but as she moved to look over his shoulder the screen suddenly changed. An email filled the screen, all about the city's Special Citizen awards ceremony.

"Sorry," he said as he turned his chair around toward her, making her back up before she lost her balance and ended up in his lap. Again. "You were saying something about some lab work?"

'Yeah, the little girl in Twenty who came in with the hundred and three temperature. Her lab work looks good. I wanted to know if I could discharge her. Are you okay?" Lacey asked, when she saw that she had lost his attention again.

"Sure, I'm fine," he said, and he rubbed his hand over his forehead as if to clear away whatever his mind had been occupied with. "Yeah, you can let her go. I've already spoken with her mother. I suspect her daughter brought home something viral from school. She should be okay by tomorrow."

"I'll have her mom call her pediatrician

if she's not better in the morning," Lacey said, and started to walk away.

"Did you get someone to cover for you for the awards ceremony?" Scott asked.

"It's taken care of. You know I wouldn't miss it," she said, as she went over to her own computer to generate the necessary paperwork for the discharge.

She looked over toward Scott as he turned back to his computer, hit some buttons, and then leaned toward the screen. He wiped at his forehead again. What was it that was bothering him? Had he just gotten that email concerning the ceremony or was it something else? They talked about pretty much everything now. If something was troubling him he knew he could talk to her.

Picking up the papers from the printer, she headed down the hallway to give a tired mother some good news and send her home to bed.

CHAPTER NINE

SCOTT LOOKED ACROSS the crowded ball-room, which tonight had been dressed up in white linen and crystal. Some of the most influential people in New Orleans had gathered there tonight, and the fact that he had been included was incredible. It was a privilege to be nominated for the city's Special Citizen award, but more importantly the attention would really help with the funding for future challenges that he was planning. The program was growing so fast that soon their annual fundraisers wouldn't be able to cover their expenses, and the last thing he wanted to do was to turn any veteran away.

He looked to where Lacey sat. She was so beautiful, sitting beside him with her hair piled up on her head. He wanted to bend toward her and kiss his way up the bare skin of her neck till he reached that one magic spot behind her ear that always made her gasp. He wanted to strip her of all her composure and expose the woman who had made love with him last night.

She chose that moment to look over at him and smile, as she laughed at something the speaker at the podium was saying. She'd worn another green dress that matched her eyes, which sparkled like emeralds with her laughter. He was so glad she was enjoying the evening— because in a few hours he'd have no choice but to ruin it.

How did he tell her that he was leaving? They'd had so little time together. Maybe they would have had a chance if this had happened later in their relationship. But now, just when she was just coming to terms with her fear of caring for someone she might suddenly lose, there was little hope that she would be waiting for him when he returned.

"Scott," Lacey said as she nudged him with her foot, "they're about to announce the nominees. Pay attention."

He forced himself to listen to the speaker as he spoke about each of the individuals nominated and their accomplishments. He recognized several of the other names, and couldn't help but be impressed that he had been nominated along with them.

When his name was announced all the people at the table where he sat clapped loudly.

"I'm so proud," said Lacey as the speaker moved on to the next nominee. "Alston was very upset when I told him only adults were invited tonight, but I reminded him of the trip to the zoo your sister is taking him on tomorrow, and he decided that the zoo would be a lot more fun than dressing up in a suit."

"Right now a trip to anywhere would be better," he said.

He really didn't like to be the center of attention. He'd rather be in the background working than have a lot of people staring at him. Lacey had made him prepare an acceptance speech, even though he knew that he wouldn't need one. She'd made him recite it to her over and over the night before, though he had told her it was a waste of time.

"And this year's winner of our New Orleans Special Citizen award is…" The man drew out the suspense while Lacey squeezed his hand. "Scott Boudreaux, founder of Extreme Warrior."

What?

He listened as the speaker read out a letter that had been sent in from one of the vets who had joined the group when she'd been at his lowest and considering suicide. Then he went on to talk about how the program had given her the confidence to make a new life in the culinary community.

Scott was shocked. It was Katie? Had she really been considering harming herself? He'd never known she was at that kind of crisis point in her life. The fact that his group of vets had helped her through that time made him proud.

The next hour went by in a blur. He stood in front of the crowd and explained the mission and vision of Extreme Warrior, and described some of their future challenges, while he tried to keep his knees from knocking behind the podium. Then he added something to his speech that he had been thinking about a lot lately but hadn't shared with Lacey.

"And while I thank you from the bottom of my heart for this honor, and your support of our local veterans, this honor really goes to my best friend and fellow officer Ben Miller, who sacrificed his life for others. This program was as much his vision as mine, and though he's been gone from us for a while now his dream of finding a way to challenge the veterans of New Orleans to be the best they can lives on in all the veterans who have taken part in this program."

He looked over at the table, where Lacey was wiping tears from her eyes.

"Thank you," he said again, then stepped down off the podium.

He shook hands with people whose names he would never remember, and was given promises of monetary support that was more than he could ever have imagined.

Lacey was working the crowd too, as if she had been born into this kind of society. He smiled as he watched her blend in with the crowd as she promoted the challenges that were planned for the program next year.

By the time they left the ballroom they were both exhausted.

For a few hours he'd forgotten that he had to tell Lacey that he was leaving. They'd both enjoyed the night and he couldn't imagine having to ruin it now. He struggled between the right thing to do and what he *wanted* to do.

The countdown of days before his departure had begun. He was running out of time. And yet something inside him rebelled against telling Lacey tonight. He wanted one more night with her. One more night to love her like she needed to be loved—one more night to show her how deep his love for her went.

As they approached her door he made his decision.

"You know, I tried that trick you were talking about? The one where you imagine everyone in the audience is in their underwear? It didn't work."

He moved in closer and turned her toward him. He bent down and kissed her neck, just above her collarbone, then ran kisses up her throat just as he had imagined earlier in the night. He'd pay the price tomorrow when he came clean with her. He'd make sure tonight was worth the pain they'd have to deal with later.

"Do you want to know why it didn't work?" he whispered into her ear, then nipped at the back of her earlobe.

"Uh-huh…" she said as she inhaled deeply and then pressed her body against his.

He didn't have her gasping yet, but the night was young.

"Because as I looked across the room the only person I had eyes for was you," he said.

He ran his hands up her neck, then entangled them in her hair, bringing his mouth to hers for a deep kiss. He poured all his longing into that kiss and then pulled back and looked into green eyes heavy with desire.

"Do you want to know what I saw?" he asked.

His body, tight with desire, begged him to take her. But if they only had this one night he was going to make it last.

"Yes…" she moaned as his lips went back to that so-sensitive spot of hers.

"I saw you there…looking so proper, with your hair piled high, your smile so sweet and innocent. Then I imagined peeling that dress off you, inch by inch, and finding that lacy pink bra..."

He ran his hands up her body and curved them around her breasts, taking the weight of them in hands.

"You know...the one that's cut down to here..."

He ran a hand down between her breasts and then moved both hands around to her back. He grasped her bottom and pulled her against the length of him.

"It has those matching panties...the ones with just that small piece of lace that hugs your bottom so tight."

Lacey moaned against him, then pulled his head down to hers. "Scott," she said between kisses, "less talking, more kissing."

He reached behind her and punched in the code for her door. Swinging the door open, he turned to Lacey and swung her up into his arms. Lacey bent her head back and laughed up at him.

Time stood still as he froze that moment into his mind. Small tendrils of hair fell around her face, framing brilliant green eyes that shone with happiness, while her bruised and swollen lips curved into a naughty smile that stole his breath. He'd thought her beautiful earlier that night, but this was the real beauty— the real Lacey. The Lacey he remembered from the first time he'd met her.

He managed to get them to the bedroom, though he stopped along the way to enjoy small tastes of her to keep him going.

How was he going to live without this woman in his life?

He made himself ignore the pain of the future. They had tonight and he wouldn't waste one moment of it.

He set her down beside the bed, then unzipped the dress and let it fall in a puddle to the floor. Standing before him in only the tiny pink bra and panties, she was sexier than his imagination could have comprehended.

Her smile turned naughty again as she peeled each piece off her body while he watched. He unbuttoned his shirt and then his pants as he tried to catch up with her.

He laid her back against the bed and took the time to freeze one more moment as he took in the vision she made stretched out before him. He'd make tonight a memory that neither of them would ever forget, no matter what tomorrow brought.

He followed her onto the bed and began to kiss her. First her lips, and then her neck, stopping at the curve of her shoulder to nip at her collarbone, then soothing the spot with a lick of his tongue before continuing his path to her breast.

"Scott..." Lacey's voice came out in a moan as she squirmed beneath him.

"Shh..." he murmured, before taking one nipple into his mouth and sucking, then moving to the next one to give it the same attention.

Then he returned to his path down her

body. He would taste every inch of her tonight…

He paused at the top of her thighs, then spread them open.

"You're killing me," Lacey said. "I can't…"

"*La petit mort, ma chérie*," he murmured as he kissed the inside of her thigh. "You will survive."

"God, I love it when you speak French," she said, then moaned again as his mouth moved higher.

Her body bucked against his mouth, and when he knew she couldn't take any more he pushed her over into her climax. Then he crawled over her and thrust inside her before her orgasm died, sending them both into that small death together.

Lacey turned the bacon and then took a long sip of coffee. She'd need a lot of caffeine to carry her through today after the night she had spent with Scott. Just thinking of their lovemaking made her heart race.

Before, she refused to call the intimacy they'd shared "lovemaking"; instead she'd preferred to think of it as simply sex. There had been no reason to bring love into it. But last night had been different. He'd made love to every part of her body. Taking his time as he tasted her, loved her, until she'd been begging him to take her. He'd stripped her of all her inhibitions, leaving her emotions bare and open to him.

She felt the flush of heat as it curled over her body along with the memories from the night before. There'd been almost a desperation in Scott that had driven him to take her over and over during the night…

"You're going to burn that if you don't turn it," Scott said as he came into the room.

She couldn't help but stare at this sexy man, dressed in wrinkled formal wear, whose eyes, still heavy with sleep, seemed to devour her with one look.

She forced her eyes away from him and removed the bacon from the frying pan.

"Good morning," she said.

Was that her voice? Just because the man looked like sex on a stick it didn't mean she needed to lose it in front of him.

She cleared her throat, then turned back toward him—only to find that he'd moved over to the coffee pot. "I've got some grits made, and there are eggs in the warming tray."

She waited for him to respond, but he seemed to be lost in thought. Had last night touched him as much as it had her? Would he tell her that he loved her now? Could she tell him that she loved him? Was that what she wanted?

He turned toward her, and the pain she saw in his eyes stopped her dead. She set the tray of bacon down on the small round table that sat to the side of the kitchen, then walked over to where he stood.

"What's wrong?" she asked. Was he ill? He did look a little pale. "Sit down. I'll get your coffee."

"I'm not sick," he said, though she noticed that he did take a chair and sit.

He might not be sick, but something was wrong. Was it her? Them? Had last night just been a lead-up to him breaking up with her?

She took the chair across from him and waited for him to tell her what was wrong. Her stomach churned with nerves as she studied him. With shoulders slumped, he stared into his coffee cup. He looked as if he'd lost his best friend—but then he'd already done that, when Ben had died. The only other person she would have considered his best friend was her, and he hadn't lost her. She was right there beside him.

Was this about the Extreme Warrior project? Was he worried about her not being able to accept his need to lead their extreme challenges? After hearing Katie's letter at last night's awards ceremony she knew she'd never be able to stop Scott from working with the veterans. She might not understand why he felt the need to take the chances he did, but he'd showed her how he worked to keep accidents and injuries from happening. He had been right when he'd said that Katie's injury could have happened anywhere. People came in all the time with snake bites from their back yard.

"I need to tell you something," he said, never looking up from his coffee. "I should have told you earlier. I just… I didn't want to ruin the time we have left together."

"I don't understand," she said.

What did he mean? Was he saying they were over? But why? She didn't understand any of this. Last night had been magical, and she knew Scott had felt that magic too. He had managed to break down every wall she'd used to protect herself from falling for him and now he wanted to end it?

Scott looked up from the table, then stood. Was he so anxious to get away from her?

"If you want to call it quits just say so," she said as her temper began to rise.

She stood and took their unused dishes to the sink. He could at least have eaten the breakfast she'd cooked for him before he broke up with her.

"I don't want to call it quits. That's the last thing I want," he said as he walked over to where she stood. "I want us to work through this. I want you to believe that I'll come back to you. I want to be enough that you're willing to take a chance on us."

She turned around to face him. She looked up into his eyes, so full of pain. And…hope?

"Just tell me what it is, Scott," she said.

He opened his arms to her and she walked into them. It felt so right, so safe to be held by him now—something that she would never have believed a few weeks ago. Whatever this problem was, they'd work through it.

She felt his chest expand as he took in a deep breath. She held on tighter to him.

"I'm being deployed back to Afghanistan. I leave in six days," he said as he rested his head on hers.

She stood there, frozen in that spot, as she tried to make sense of his words.

Scott had finished his time in the military.

How could they make him go back to Afghanistan?

It didn't make any sense at all.

She let her hands slide down his back, then took a step away from him. She needed to understand what he was saying.

"You've been out of the military for three years now. They can't make you go back into service," she said. "Besides, you were injured. The damage to your leg was extensive."

"And it has healed now. I climb mountains and my leg holds up fine," he said.

"It still gives you trouble. You still limp when you've pushed yourself too hard. You should tell them about the limp. You should make them see that you can't be expected to be deployed again. Just tell them you're not going."

She heard the terror in her voice. She couldn't be expected to sit at home again, waiting for the doorbell to ring. Waiting for the army chaplain to tell her that Scott had been killed. Waiting for her life to be destroyed once again.

She'd wanted to scream at the men who had come to her house the day Ben had been killed. She'd wanted to tell them to shut up, to leave and never come back, but she'd known she couldn't. She'd had to be strong. She'd had to be brave. She'd had to be there for Alston and for Ben's parents.

"It's only for six months, Lacey. One of the doctors has become ill and has had to be flown home for surgery. They're working short-handed right now, and they need me to cover until he's recovered."

"Why can't you just tell them no?" she said.

She didn't know what to say to him to make him understand. She couldn't do this again.

"I only served four years. I had four years left of inactive reserves. By the end of this deployment my eight years will be completed and I won't have to worry about getting called up again. We just need to make it through those six months. They really need me, Lacey. It's hard enough in the hospitals over there without them being short. I have to go."

But she needed him too. How could he expect her to go through this again?

She thought of the days she'd lain in bed, too depressed to get up and get dressed. She had functioned the best she could, to make sure Alston was taken care of, but she hadn't been the kind of mother she'd wanted to be. It had only been when Scott had come home and helped her get her act together that she'd seen just what a lousy job she was doing.

She couldn't put herself and Alston through that again. She'd been through hell when she'd lost Ben and she couldn't do it again.

She felt panic rise up inside her as her heart sped up. She turned and gripped the side of the counter and forced herself to take the deep, calming breaths she needed to fight it down.

"I know I don't have the right to ask this of you, but I can't just walk away from you. I love you, Lacey. I want us to be together forever. I want to make a real family with you and Alston. I just need you to believe in us. Give us a chance."

She felt the tears as they rolled down her cheeks and then suddenly she was sobbing. It was as if she had lost Ben all over again, but instead of Ben it was now Scott she was losing. She wanted to believe that Scott would come home, but she couldn't. There was no guarantee that he would come back to her and she could not live with the fear of losing him.

"I can't do it, Scott. I'm sorry."

She turned around and threw herself in his arms and held him tight. If only she could hold on to him forever. If only she never had to let him go.

She pushed herself away from him, then ran from the room. Closing the bedroom door behind her, she curled up on the bed. She buried her head in the covers and breathed in the scent of Scott and cried.

CHAPTER TEN

"WHERE'S THAT TRAUMA BLOOD?" Scott asked as he quickly examined the gunshot victim lying on the trauma table.

The kid couldn't be over nineteen. He was just a boy. What could he have done to get himself shot?

They'd stripped him down at the scene and he could see two entrance wounds in the chest.

"We need to turn him over," he shouted to the nurse beside him.

Where was Lacey? There were too many inexperienced nurses in the room. She was in charge. She should be there to help.

He examined the kid's back and saw that there was only one exit wound. He would need to go to surgery. His job until the surgeon arrived was to stabilize the patient, and with the amount of blood this kid had lost it was going to take this whole team to do it.

"I've got the blood," one of the younger nurses called as she walked into the room carrying a red cooler.

"It should have been here five minutes ago. Let's get it going," he said as he looked up at the monitor.

He was tachycardic, and his blood pressure was low, but it was holding. If they could get some blood into him he might make it.

"Where's X-ray?" he shouted across the room.

He watched as a young man pushed the machine into the room. Could he move any slower? Didn't he understand that this kid was going to die if they didn't get him stabilized soon?

He backed out of the room with the rest of the staff while the X-ray was taken, then quickly returned to the patient's side and checked out the screen on the X-ray machine.

"It looks like one of the bullets hit his left lung. He's going to need a chest tube."

"His oxygen saturation is dropping," the respiratory technician said.

"So is his pressure," said one of the nurses.

Scott looked up to see the pressure had dropped down to eighty over forty-four.

"Is the blood going? Where's Lacey?" he asked. "We need that blood going or we're going to lose him."

"I'm over here," he heard Lacey say.

He looked over to where she and another one of the nurses were setting up the blood to rapidly infuse.

"The blood is starting now," Lacey said.

"His oxygen stats are still dropping," the respiratory tech told him.

"Where's that chest tube tray?" he said.

"It's right here, Doctor," Lacey said beside him.

There was no missing the censure in

her voice. Yeah, he knew he was being a jerk, but right now all that mattered was saving this kid.

He gowned, and then prepped the incision site. After making the incision he inserted the chest tube, then began to stitch it in place.

He couldn't help but remember that night when he'd stood in a room just down the hall, when that drunk had grabbed the scalpel and held Lacey hostage. Just thinking about that night made him angry. Not just at the drunk, but at himself too.

He should never have kissed Lacey that night. No, that was the anger and pain in him talking. If he had it all to do over he knew he'd kiss her again.

The young kid's vital signs began to stabilize as they continued to transfuse him with multiple units of blood. As soon as the trauma surgeon arrived to take him to Theater, Scott left the room. In a few days he'd be back in Afghanistan, taking care of patients just like that kid, and some of them wouldn't be much older.

Lacey tried to ignore the rest of the staff as they gathered at the unit coordinator's desk and gossiped. She'd seen the looks some of the staff were giving her. Everyone was wondering what was wrong with Scott and they all assumed that she knew.

Of course she knew. The man was about to leave the States and return to the place where he'd lost his best friend. It wouldn't be easy for him to do that. And then there was the issue of the two of them—though if anyone understood why she couldn't deal with the danger he was going to be in, it was him. He'd seen her at her lowest, with an empty bottle of alcohol at her side. And he'd stayed by her as she'd crawled her way back up, she reminded herself.

"I just talked to Dr. MacDonald. He says that Scott is being redeployed to Afghanistan. He turned in his notice today," one of the respiratory techs was telling the group.

"Well, that sucks," one of the new nurses said. "Don't they have to hold your job open for you if you're deployed?"

"Dr. MacDonald said Scott told him he wasn't sure what he wanted to do when he returned, so he decided to turn his resignation in."

Lacey couldn't help but look over at the group. Why would Scott turn in his resignation? He loved his job working in the ER at the hospital. Was it because of her? They'd worked together before they'd ever become romantically involved, so that didn't make any sense.

"Don't you have something to do? You know…something like taking care of your patients?" the unit coordinator said.

"Thanks, Gloria," said Lacey, when the crowd broke up.

"No problem," the older woman said, then returned to her computer. "Maybe you could go talk to him? He's been impossible to work with for the last two days. I'm thinking there might be a mutiny if he doesn't stop biting everyone's head off."

"Where is he?" Lacey asked.

She'd take this one for the team. It was her responsibility as charge nurse to make sure everything ran smoothly in the department.

And this has nothing to do with the fact that I'm worried about him.

"He went into the doctors' lounge," Gloria said.

Knowing that she was the last person he'd want to see, she prepared herself. This was the problem with dating someone that you worked with. Things had a tendency to cross over between your personal and your private life if you weren't careful. They'd crossed that line the first time Scott had kissed her, and now they were paying the price.

Scott sat at the table, holding a soft drink in one hand while the other one tapped a beat on the table. He looked up and scowled as she walked into the room.

"You don't have to tell me. I was being a jerk in the trauma room and I owe everyone an apology," he said. "I've got it. You can go now."

"You were, and you do, but that isn't the only reason I need to talk to you," she said.

She saw the glint of hope in his eyes when he looked at her, and then it was gone. She was relieved that he had accepted her decision to end their romantic relationship. She'd explained her reasons for not continuing and she was glad he wasn't pushing back at her.

If only it didn't hurt so much to see him like this.

"What happened out there, Scott? That wasn't you," she said.

"I don't know. It was just that kid. He's so young—too young. He reminded me of all the kids I treated in Afghanistan. There were some like him—the lucky ones, who managed to survive—but there were just as many who didn't," he said. He ran his hands through his hair, then looked up at her. "And next week I'll be right back in the middle of things, trying to save the ones I can and having to deal with the reality of those I can't."

"I'm sorry," she said. "I don't want you to go. I wish—"

"What do you wish?" Scott said as he stood and moved toward her.

He ran a hand down the side of her face, and she wanted to turn to him but knew she couldn't.

"I wish I was different," she said as she stepped away from him.

Just two steps, but it felt as if she had run a marathon. It was so hard to walk away from Scott. If only she wasn't such a coward.

"The rumor is that you're not coming back here after you return from deployment. Is it true?" she asked as she took another step away from him.

If she was the reason he was leaving she had to stop him. She couldn't let that happen. She could easily get a job at another hospital. Besides, it had been Scott who got her the job working here, after she'd finally gotten her act together after Ben's death. If one of them left it should be her.

"I'm leaving all my options open right now," he said as he walked over to the recycling bin and threw away his empty drink can.

"If it's because of me, I can leave. It's not right that you have to give up your job," she said.

Why did this have to hurt so badly? But how much more would it hurt if she waited for Scott to return while all the time knowing that he might never make it home alive?

"There's no reason for you to do that. I've been thinking about making a change for a while now. This deployment has just changed the timing of things," he said as he opened the door and they both stepped out into the emergency room.

As they went their separate ways she felt the pain of knowing that Scott was already moving on and making plans for a future without her.

But that was what she wanted.

No, it wasn't what she wanted.

She wanted things to go back to the way they used to be. The way things had been before that one kiss changed everything.

Lacey opened her eyes to find her son making a goofy face, crossing his eyes and twisting his mouth into a crazy rendition of a smile. Laughing, she pulled him into the bed beside her and tickled him.

As his laughter filled the room she remembered a time when she would have rolled away from him in the bed, too tired and too depressed to play with her little boy. This kid and his crazy antics meant everything to her. That was why she knew she could never take the chance of being pulled back into that deep hole she'd fallen into after losing Ben. She needed the security of knowing that she and Alston wouldn't have to go through that torment again.

"Did you get your paper done?" she asked as she got out of bed and yawned, then headed to get dressed. Working the night shift was hard on the body but it worked well with Alston's school schedule.

"I need some help with my science," he said as she came out of the bathroom, where she had changed clothes.

"Okay, let's look at it," she said as they walked toward the kitchen. "What's it about?"

"We're working on our science projects. I'm doing parachutes, so I've got to write a paper on gravity." Alston said as he pulled a notebook from his backpack.

"Well, that sounds really interesting, but I don't know much about parachutes. Are you sure you want to do this for your project? We could find you one that I could help you with. What about something with seeds?"

"I only need some help with this first part," Alston said. "Scott's going to help me with the rest of it. Did you know he jumped out of a plane once? He knows all about parachutes."

Lacey felt her heart drop into her stomach. She'd forgotten that Alston didn't know about Scott's deployment. She'd have to tell him today. Or should she call Scott and let *him* tell her son? No, she was being a coward again. She would have to do it.

"How about we walk down to the library and see what books we can find on gravity?" she said.

The walk would be good for both of them. And it would give her a chance to tell her son that Scott was leaving. Maybe they would find another subject for his science project while they were at the library…

"That would be awesome. Can we get some ice cream too?" he asked.

"Sure. We'll have to stop for ice cream on the way back, though. I don't think the librarians would want us touching their books with sticky hands."

As Alston ran off to get his shoes she tried to think of the best way to tell her son that Scott would be leaving in a couple days. The two of them had a special relationship that shouldn't end over her and Scott's split. She knew Scott would never let that happen, though she would need to explain to Alston the change in her and Scott's relationship.

She'd spent so much time worrying about moving on and leaving Ben behind. But then she'd taken her first step toward a future with Scott and realized she wasn't moving on without Ben—she was just moving forward and taking his memory with her.

Scott had been the one to show her that she could do that. It had been when he had explained to the crowd at the awards banquet how Ben was still a part of the veteran program that it had hit her that moving on didn't mean leaving Ben behind.

And now that she was finally ready to see where the future could take them he was leaving—and she was too much of a coward to wait for him.

As they walked the ten blocks to the local library the constant jabber of her son lightened her heart—until she remembered that she would soon have to tell him about Scott's deployment.

Alston had been only five when his father had been killed, and with the resiliency of a child he had accepted the change in his life more easily than she had expected. There had been nights, though, right after Ben had first been killed, when she'd found him crying in his bed when he should have been asleep, but she blamed that on the fact that she had been too caught up in her own grieving to see the pain her son had been hiding from her.

Alston quickly found some books on gravity, and they spent the next hour putting together a paper.

She told herself that it was the cool temperature of the library and being surrounded by books that made her drag out the time as they went through the shelves of books, looking for something to read after they'd finished the paper, but she knew she was just postponing the inevitable.

Not for the first time she considered backing out and having Scott tell her son that he was leaving, but she couldn't do it. Alston was her son, and she needed to be the one to break the news to him.

As they crossed the street from the ice cream store she took Alston's hand in hers while they both licked their melting cones.

"Mom, I can walk by myself," Alston whined. "You treat me like a baby."

"You *are* a baby. You're *my* baby," she

said as she licked at a drip of ice cream running down her cone.

She might be a little more protective than some of Alston's friends' parents, but with all the things she saw in the ER, and after losing Ben, she felt she had the right to be a little paranoid.

"I'm almost nine. That is not a baby," Alston said as he tried to pull away from her.

They'd almost made it onto the sidewalk when she heard the loud racing of an engine. She looked up and saw a car speed through the red light and head straight for them.

Letting go of Alston, she pushed him toward the sidewalk.

The last thing she saw was her son hitting the concrete—and then there was just pain.

Scott rushed into the emergency room. He'd been in the process of going through his pantry, to dispose of everything that wouldn't be edible when he returned from deployment, when his phone had suddenly been flooded with text messages.

Assuming all the messages coming in were good wishes from people who had heard about his departure, he'd finished disposing of the food items into the trash before he'd picked up his phone.

He'd read the first text message, from one of the nurses in the emergency room at the hospital, and then gone on to the next message. None of it had made any sense. There had to be some type of mistake.

But when his phone had begun to ring and the caller ID had identified the hospital he'd grabbed his keys.

A hospital social worker had explained that there had been an accident and that as he was listed as Alston's next of kin they needed him to come.

"But what about his mother? Where is she?" he'd asked, even as he'd started his car and headed to the hospital.

After being told several times that she wasn't able to give any information concerning a patient's condition over the phone, he'd hung up and called the ER directly. When Gloria had answered she'd put him through to the ER doctor taking care of Alston.

He had listened carefully as the doctor had explained that Alston had fallen and had a radius fracture that would require a cast. He'd been pulling into the parking lot when the doctor had gone on to tell him that while the kid was going to be fine, Lacey had been brought in as a trauma and was being cared for by one of the other doctors.

None of it had made sense to his muddled mind. Alston had fallen, but Lacey had been brought into the hospital too.

By the time he made it to the trauma room it was empty. Empty packages littered the floor, along with blood-stained clothes. Recognizing the bloody shirt that declared the wearer a unicorn nurse, he headed to the doctors' station.

Someone was going to explain to him what was happening.

"Dr. Boudreaux," Gloria said, "thank goodness you're here. This is just awful. Alston is worried to death about his mother and we didn't know what you would want us to tell him."

"Gloria, I need you to tell me what happened." Scott made himself stop and take a breath. "Where exactly is Lacey?"

He listened to the unit coordinator as she told him everything she knew. There'd been an accident—pedestrian versus motor vehicle. They'd brought both Lacey and Alston in by ambulance, but Lacey was the one who had been struck by the car and her injuries were more serious.

He tracked down the nurse taking care of Lacey, only to learn that she had been rushed off to surgery due to internal bleeding.

He wanted to bust into the operating

room and take over the case. It was at times like this when he wished he'd remained in surgery. But after Afghanistan he'd thought that working in an ER would give him a break. Now he was thinking of making more changes in his life—but none of it would matter if he lost Lacey.

Returning to the ER, he hunted down Alston's room. The boy rushed at Scott when he saw him and then he began to cry.

"Whoa, now," Scott said as he carefully supported the boy's arm, which was sporting a new blue cast.

"Have you seen her?" Alston asked when Scott had picked him up and put him up on the examining table.

A bright red scratch cut down across one side of the kid's face, but it wasn't deep and wouldn't scar.

"Not yet. She's in the operating room. But I made someone call inside the room and the doctor said she was doing better," Scott said as he examined the boy for any other injuries, even though he knew a thorough examination would have been done when Alston had first arrived.

"Hey, Scott," said a nurse dressed in a pair of bright pink scrubs, who was sitting in the corner. "Alston has been cleared by the doctor to be discharged. We were just waiting for you to arrive."

"Thank you, Amanda," Scott told the woman.

"I'll have them bring in the paperwork," she said as she left the room.

"Do you remember what happened?" Scott asked Alston.

"We went to the library to get some information for my science project. You know—the one on parachutes that you're going to help me do," Alston said.

The boy flinched as he moved his arm as if to make the shape of a parachute. Scott would have to see if they could get some pain medication for him before he was discharged. And the science project...

Scott had forgotten all about his promise to help Alston with the parachute assignment. Had Lacey explained to the boy that he was leaving?

"What happened when you left the library?" Scott asked.

"Well," Alston said, "we went to get ice cream after we left the hospital, but we didn't stay at the store to eat it. Momma said that she had to talk to me about something on the way home and we could eat it while we walked. And then, just while we were crossing the road—and we crossed with the light, like Momma says you have to—this car came *speeding* up."

Scott backed away as Alston swung the arm with the cast around, indicating a car speeding past.

"And then Momma pushed me and I landed on the sidewalk."

As the boy took a breath after telling his story, Scott tried to piece together all the information.

"Then some people came up to me and they wouldn't let me see my mom."

Alston began to cry and Scott picked him up and hugged him. The kid had been through a lot already today, falling and breaking his arm, and now he was separated from his mother.

"As soon as your mom gets out of surgery the two of us will go see her—okay?" Scott promised him.

"She's really going to be okay?" Alston asked as he wiped his eyes and nose against Scott's shirt.

"I know the doctor doing the surgery and he said your mom is doing well. Now, I'm going to make some phone calls and see if you can go stay with Jason tonight. Is that okay with you?" Scott said.

"That's okay—but not until after I see my mom," Alston said.

After Scott had made some calls to his family, then to Lacey's mother in Florida, he found the nurse and asked for some medication for Alston's pain, then signed the discharge paperwork.

The two of them were quickly joined in the waiting room by Scott's mother and father, who had offered to take Alston to Jason's house after they'd made sure Lacey was going to be okay.

By the time Lacey's surgeon came out of the operating room Alston had fallen asleep. Picking up the boy, Scott carried him down the hall to the recovery room, where Scott had been given special permission to see Lacey.

"Alston, wake up," Scott said as he shook the boy awake. "Here's your mom. She's sleepy like you are…see?"

The boy opened his eyes and looked over at his mother. "She's really going to be okay?" Alston asked.

"She's really going to be okay. She just needs a nap right now," Scott told him. "I'm going to stay with her for the night, and if anything changes I'll call you. Okay?"

"Okay. Can I go to Jason's now?" Alston asked.

"Sure," Scott said, and he carried him back out to the waiting room.

CHAPTER ELEVEN

LACEY AWOKE TO the chattering of her son—something that didn't surprise her. She stretched, and it did surprise her to find an intravenous line in her arm.

Turning toward her son, she saw the bright blue cast on his arm and slowly the memory of the car speeding toward them returned—and with it fear for her son.

"Alston…" she said, her voice coming out in a croak as she tried to sit up and go to her son.

"He's okay," Scott said from the side of the bed.

Alston bounced over to her.

"Remember I told you she'd be sore after the surgery? We have to be careful not to touch her where she has that dressing on her stomach. We have to be very careful where she has that line in her arm too," Scott reminded her son.

"Sorry," Alston said, and he moved closer to her, then patted her hand gently.

"He's really okay?" she asked Scott as she ran her free hand over the large scrape on his face.

"I talked to one of the cops who worked the scene. The car was being driven by a high school kid who was paying more attention to his radio than to his driving. If you hadn't pushed Alston out of the way… Let's just say it would have ended differently," Scott said.

"The cop said you saved my life, Momma. You're a hero, just like Scott— only you haven't gotten an award," Alston said, then turned to Scott. "I think we should go buy my mom a trophy. One of those big ones, like we won when we beat that soccer team last year—you know the guys with those ugly green uniforms."

"We'll have to see what they have in the gift shop. Why don't I take you down?"

When the nurse came in to give Lacey her pain medication, Scott took Alston downstairs to wait for Rayanne.

Scott had explained the circumstances of the accident as had been told to him by the police officer he had spoken to, but Lacey still couldn't understand what had happened. She'd just taken her son out for a trip to the library and an ice cream cone. It had been a spontaneous trip, a few blocks down the street from their house. Alston had said that they'd waited for the light, checked for cars, and stayed on the walkway that crossed the street.

She'd almost been killed doing something as innocent and safe as going to the library.

Scott had been right. You could get killed just as easily crossing the street as you could climbing a mountain.

Or working at a hospital in Afghanistan?

No, that was different. Scott would be in a lot more danger than she would ever be crossing a street. But did that mean she couldn't accept that risk?

She had to make a decision. She'd survived being hit by a speeding car. She'd been given a second chance. But was she brave enough to face a future with Scott in Afghanistan?

Alston had called her a hero. If he only knew what a coward his mother really was. It was as if she could see happiness just beyond her reach, but was too scared to grab it.

If Ben could have picked a man out for her and Alston she knew it would have been Scott. The man who had been there for her when she hadn't thought she could go on. But she was afraid to be there for him while he used his medical knowledge to take care of others. What kind of friend did that make her?

Scott stopped outside Lacey's hospital room and prepared himself. He was set to leave the next day, and this would be the last chance he'd have to see her before he left.

He heard a sound through the door that sounded like someone was crying, and pushed open the door. Lacey was sitting up in the bed while she cried into the covers.

Moving to the bed, he eased her into his arms. "It's okay," he said. "Is it the pain? I'll call the doctor and get your medicine increased if you're still hurting."

"It's not the pain," Lacey said. "It's me. I've been such a coward."

"You're not a coward. You're one of the bravest people I know," Scott said.

He rested his chin on her head and breathed in the sweet scent of her. He'd miss that scent while he was gone.

"No, I'm not. And I've been an awful friend, too," she said. "I've been totally irrational concerning everything. And I could have been killed just walking to the library."

He tried to understand what it was that

she was saying, but she was beginning to ramble like her eight-year-old son.

"It's just the pain medication," he told her. "As soon as you get some rest you'll feel better."

"No, I won't," she said. "I've messed things up, and now you're leaving, and I didn't even get a chance to tell you that I love you."

"I love you too," Scott said, knowing that she wouldn't understand that he meant it in a purely *un*-platonic way.

"No," Lacey said as she drew away from him. "I *love* you, Scott. As in I'm *in love* with you."

Scott stepped away from the bed. With all the pain medication she had been given, did she even know what she was saying?

"You've had a hard day, Lacey. They've given you a lot of medication to help with the pain. We can talk about this after you take a nap," Scott said.

"It's not the medication. I know how I feel," Lacey said, then yawned.

Scott watched as Lacey's eyes closed and her respirations became even. Did she really know how she felt? Did she truly know how *he* felt?

He'd asked her to wait for him but he'd never come out and asked her if she would *marry* him. He'd been afraid that he'd scare her off if he asked too much of her, too fast, but he'd assumed that she must know where he was hoping the relationship would eventually go.

Lacey opened her eyes and looked across the room to where Scott sat in a chair, asleep. Had she really told him that she loved him or had it all been a drug-induced dream?

She lay in the bed and watched him. Drugs or no drugs, she knew what she wanted now. There'd be no more wasting her life. She'd spent too much time letting her fear of the unknown keep her from admitting her feelings for Scott. She wouldn't let him leave without telling him how she really felt.

He stirred in the chair, then looked over at her. "Do you feel better?" he asked.

"Yes. Can you come over here?" she asked as she moved over on the bed. "We need to talk."

"Sure," he said, and he stood and moved closer to the bed. "Look, I want you to know that I understand that you might not have meant everything you said earlier. I don't want you to think that I'm holding you to it. Pain medication can do funny things to people."

"Which things are you talking about?" she asked.

"Well, you said that you love me," Scott said.

"Yes, I did," she said.

"You said that you were *in* love with me," Scott said.

"Yes, I did," she said.

"And you said that you would marry

me when I came back to the States," he said, his lips turned up into a mischievous smile.

"Scott Boudreaux—I never said any such thing. Besides, you didn't ask me to marry you," Lacey said as she pushed herself up in the bed.

"Lacey, will you marry me when I get back?" Scott asked.

He looked so hopeful, and she knew inside her heart that she was making the right decision for both of them.

"No, I won't marry you when you come back. But I will marry you before you leave."

She laughed as Scott collapsed back into the chair beside the bed.

"Are you okay?" she asked.

"Are you sure? I don't even have a ring for you," Scott said as he took her hand in his.

"I'm sure. That is if it's what you want?" she said.

She hadn't considered that he might want a big wedding.

"It's what I want. But how are we going to make it work? I leave tomorrow night!" Scott said.

"Well, the first thing we need to do is call your mother and your sisters," Lacey told him. "If anyone can get a wedding together by then it would be your family."

It took them more than a day, but with a change in flight and some phone calls Scott managed to get an extra day—which also allowed Lacey a little more time to recover in the hospital before she was whisked off to his parents' house by his sisters.

Instead of the usual bachelor party, Scott and Alston spent the night playing video games and eating pizza. According to Alston it was the best bachelor party ever.

Scott had felt it was important for him to get Alston's approval, but he hadn't been prepared for Alston's simple answer when he had asked the boy if he could marry his mother.

"I think my daddy would want you to marry my mom," Alston said.

"You do? Why is that?" Scott had asked.

"Well, my daddy loved you. And my daddy loved my mother. Doesn't that mean that he'd want you two to love each other?"

And that was that, as far as the eight-year-old boy was concerned. And Scott couldn't help but feel that Alston was right. That somehow Ben had had a part in him and Lacey falling in love.

As a surprise, Scott had managed to get the management of Baby Blues to open early, and his sisters had set up the courtyard there for the ceremony. He remembered how Lacey had loved the magical feel of the place. They might not have had a lot of time to plan the wedding, but they were only going to do this once and he wanted to make sure they did it right.

Now, pacing back and forth, Scott waited at the entrance, watching for the car he'd rented to arrive. As it turned in he stepped back and waited. When the car came to a stop, Scott opened the door before the driver could come around.

Lacey stepped out and the courtyard went silent. She wore a simple white dress that left her shoulders bare.

Louis Armstrong sang "A Kiss to Build a Dream On" over the speakers—the song he had requested. It would be their song from now on, and he could imagine it playing forty years from now, as they danced together with their arthritic joints and graying hair.

"It's all so beautiful," she said as she looked around the courtyard.

"Are you ready to get married?" Scott asked her.

"I'm ready," she answered as she slipped her hand into his. "I'm finally ready."

EPILOGUE

SCOTT STARED STRAIGHT ahead and reminded himself that he couldn't embarrass his wife. He'd spent his life taking on some of the most dangerous challenges around the world. He'd hiked the Alaskan mountains and dived in shark cages. He'd parachuted out of planes and been white water rafting on some of the fastest rivers in the world. But nothing had ever scared him like what he saw on the ultrasound machine.

"There are two of them?" he said for the third time.

"Yes," said the ultrasound technician. "There are two."

"And they're both girls?" he said, again for the third time.

"Yes," his wife and the ultrasound technician said both together. "They're both girls."

"But there are two?" he said as he turned to his wife. "We're going to have two girls? At the same time?"

"That's usually how it works with twins," his wife told him as the technician wiped the gel from her stomach.

How could she be so calm about this? Of course, in his defense, she had known about this for longer than he had. He'd been overseas when Lacey had learned they were having twins, and she had sneakily kept that information to herself.

He watched as the technician printed out a picture, then handed it to his wife.

"Here—hold this," Lacey said, and she pushed him down to sit on the table and handed him the picture. Then she pulled out her phone and snapped a photo of him.

"What was that for?" he asked as he looked down at the picture in his hand.

"I just wanted to make sure I got a photo

of something I never thought I'd see," Lacey said.

"What?" he asked as he stood to follow her out of the room.

"I think, Dr. Scott Boudreaux, you have finally found your most extreme challenge," his wife said, then strolled out of the room, following the technician.

And, looking down at the picture in his hand, of the two little girls who would soon join his family, he had to admit that she was right.

* * * * *

LET'S TALK
Romance

For exclusive extracts, competitions
and special offers, find us online:

- **f** facebook.com/millsandboon
- ⓞ @millsandboonuk
- 🐦 @millsandboon

Or get in touch on 0844 844 1351*

For all the latest titles coming soon,
visit millsandboon.co.uk/nextmonth

*Calls cost 7p per minute plus your phone company's price per
minute access charge

Want even more
ROMANCE?

Join our bookclub today!